The Lost, the Found
And the Hidden

The Puzzle Box Chronicles: Book 2

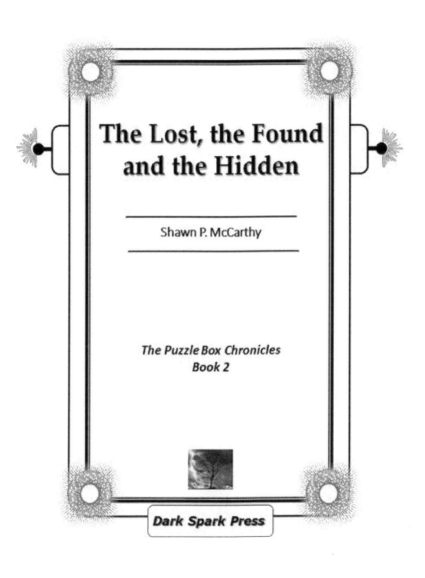

The Lost, the Found and the Hidden

Shawn P. McCarthy

The Puzzle Box Chronicles
Book 2

Dark Spark Press

Book cover design by Teodora Chinde
Printed in the United States of America
First Printing, 2016
ISBN-13: 978-0996896719 (Dark Spark Press)
ISBN-10: 0996896716

Dark Spark Press

www.DarkSparkPress.com

Publisher.DarkSparkPress@gmail.com

For

Mary McCarthy

Introduction to Book 2

What happens when the end of one life triggers profound changes in another?

The Lost, the Found and the Hidden: The Puzzle Box Chronicles Book 2 picks up where Book 1, *Wreck of the Gossamer* left off.

... -- ...   ... -- ...   ... -- ...   ... -- ...

In many ways, the last decade of the 19th century marked the beginning of our modern era.

In rapid succession, the United States saw an expansion in the availability of electricity, the availability of affordable telephone service and the fledgling emergence of the auto industry. It also saw a huge increase in trans-Atlantic ship traffic and the ability of average citizens to see and experience things in a way that previously had only been available to the wealthy.

As we saw in Book 1. .

Into these final years of the Gilded Age sails Victor Marius, an inspired scientist and budding entrepreneur. This is an era of burgeoning science, technology and business, and it is perfectly suited for him. Unfortunately, Victor is lost in a shipwreck off the coast of Cape Cod in the summer of 1891. But, before he disappears, he manages to release a strange box that he hopes will protect his legacy.

Amanda Malcom, a young woman enduring a troubled marriage, is about to make a mysterious discovery on a Cape Cod beach that will lead her on a dangerous odyssey – one that eventually takes her across the country, and into the heart of a rapidly changing America. Along the way, she meets Plains Indians, ex-slaves, riverboat charlatans, and secretive workers who champion the U.S. labor movement.

At a time when electric lighting is spreading across the country like a wave, she also meets inspired engineers and even Montana miners who dig deep to feed the country's insatiable demand for copper. Amanda has survived many things in her short life, but it's not clear if she will be able to survive the first year of the last decade of the 19th century.

Shawn P. McCarthy

Chapter 1

Steam

Late June, 1891
Boston, Massachusetts

Dawn in the city arrives in slumber and a quiet tolerance, which lingers until an urban urgency takes delivery of the day.

In a place like Boston, predawn is a transitional world that lives for barely an hour. It has a language all its own, made up of soft background noise and a jumble of tastes and smells. It's a communiqué of sound and gesture, basked in gold light.

Not everyone understands the language of the early dawn. Milkmen certainly speak it. Their horse carts rattle through empty alleys. Street sweepers and ice men silently nod hello. Morning birds speak the language too. Perched on smokeless summer chimneys, they run through their book of songs. Even policemen speak it as they saunter back toward their station houses, lost in quiet solitude.

Into this peaceful time, a new sound arrives in Boston. It interrupts the quiet morning with a tattered hiss of steam and a rumble of iron-clad wooden wheels – wheels that have become wobbly and misshapen during a bumpy trip. Like a long loud drum roll, this sound awakens other morning dwellers. Heads turn to see what's causing the roar.

Amanda Malcolm steams into the city's South End. She clutches the controls of her ancient Dudgeon steam car and looks straight ahead, ignoring the stares of the few people she passes on the street. Is she doing something wrong by driving this mechanical beast? Maybe even illegal? She doesn't know. Making eye contact might mean having to explain herself.

As she reaches the more crowded parts of the city, she eases back on the speed lever and steers the Dudgeon carefully through the narrow streets. The cobblestones are a bad match for the wagon, making it feel like she's sitting atop her own personal earthquake.

Eyes wide, street pedestrians quickly step back onto the curb as she passes. Goggles are pushed back above her forehead now. Scarf blown askew and hair wrenched out from under its combs, everything seems to waft behind her like a bird losing its feathers.

She clicks the speed lever down again and makes a tight turn, ignoring a man who calls to her from a shop window. Then she slides the lever back up again, moving faster into the broader and newer downtown avenues. Newspaper boys try to chase the steam engine but can't keep up. She understands now why Elmer Quincy told her to arrive before dawn. It's after sunrise now and she's already become a curiosity.

Dogs bark at her wheels as she turns onto Hanover Street, climbing up into the North End. The hissing and clanking takes her down gravel side streets. She makes two loops before finding the correct address.

Afraid to just shut the machine down in the middle of the street, she turns into an alley and glides toward the back gate of the large home she's trying to reach. It stands open, so she rumbles into the tiny yard. Had she been riding a horse, she'd just close the gate and let it graze. But what is one supposed to do with a steam wagon? Yanking back on the lever, she disengages the drive train and lets the machine idle. In less than a minute, she sees heads popping over a nearby fence. More people stare from the houses across the alley. *Keep a low profile,* Elmer told her.

She probably shouldn't just sit in the yard. Noticing that the door to the home's carriage house is unlocked, she climbs down, flings it open, and runs back to the wagon. She'll drive it inside, and hide the wagon. The pride and skill she feels at pulling the wagon gently through the small opening quickly turns to surprise as the building fills with dark smoke. Realizing her mistake, she fights with the gearshift. But she can't find a way to make the wagon back up. Can this thing even go backwards?

Coughing and blinking, Amanda disengages the drive, sets the brake, and releases the steam. She gasps for air and stumbles out of the building toward a water pump that stands atop a block of cement in the backyard. Finding a pair of wooden buckets, she pumps by hand, fills them with water and lurches back into the carriage house. Holding her breath against the smoke, she douses the fire beneath the boiler. It hisses terribly and spits white ash at her. Eyes watering, she empties the second bucket too.

Wiping her face with her skirt, she steps from the brick garage through a cloud of steam, smoke, and ash, like Aphrodite emerging from a boiling sea. Her cheeks are streaked with sweat, tears, and soot, and her dress is as filthy as a street urchin's.

A man and a woman, wide-eyed and bemused, stand in the center of the yard, staring at her ghostly figure. The man finally speaks. "Mrs. Malcolm, I presume?"

Amanda nods, brushing wet hair away from her forehead. Remembering her manners, she steps forward and extends her hand. "Mr. ... Mr. Morgan?"

A crowd of people wander through the back gate, and two boys peer into the smoky carriage house.

The man laughs. "We've been expecting you. Though we didn't expect you to arrive quite ... like this." He ignores the grime and shakes her hand while Mrs. Morgan mumbles something about Elmer Quincy's love of contraptions.

"I ... I really am sorry." Amanda gestures toward the carriage house. "I didn't think it would ... I mean ...."

"Nonsense. Don't worry about it, dear," the woman finally speaks up. "No harm done. I'm Beverly, and this is my husband, Jonathan. He's been excited about your arrival ever since he got the telegram saying you'd borrowed Elmer's crazy wagon. I suspect you won't see much of my husband for the rest of the day. Once that thing cools down, he'll be out here trying to figure out how it works."

They help Amanda into the house and to a washroom. A basin and fresh pitcher of water stand atop a copper-clad dry sink. Beverly loans Amanda a skirt and blouse. In fifteen minutes, the young woman emerges looking like a completely different person. Soon she finds herself sitting in a small kitchen nook, enjoying tea with honey toast and recounting her adventures on the open road. They gasp when she says she reached a terrifying speed that had to be over thirty miles per hour!

"Well, dear," Beverly says as she clears the dishes, "you've been up all night on quite the adventure. You should get some rest." She looks the girl up and down, surprised at just how delicate yet athletic she looks in her clean clothes.

But Amanda isn't tired at all. She wants to look around, and to maybe visit the neighborhood where she grew up. It's only about ten blocks away, northwest toward the river. There's no way she can sleep. Not this morning. The only part of her that feels tired is her hands—from gripping the levers so tightly.

Chapter 2

Southeast

Outskirts of Boston

Earlier that night

In the last car of a six-coach passenger train, Jeb Thomas has drifted off to sleep. As the locomotive begins its decent down a small hill, about six miles south of Boston, its whistle blows, signaling the train's approach to the Quincy station. The noise startles Jeb – enough to make him jump. His leg, stretched out on the empty seat beside him, slips off. That weight shift pulls him forward, and the noise of his foot hitting the floor causes him to jump again. Eyes wide open now and heart racing, he realizes what has happened. Chuckling, he rubs his eyes.

Awake now, he gazes out the window and sees a nearly deserted station slide into view. The train slows. The conductor steps down and disappears into the building.

Jeb does a full-body stretch, then walks out onto the station platform. The night is cool.

He paces a bit.

Rolls a cigarette.

In the distance there are outlines of buildings, but at this hour lamplight is missing from the windows. He drags the smoke into his lungs and exhales slowly, looking at the stars.

Jeb has a long history of traveling on trains at 2 a.m. As a labor organizer he's learned to slip into and out of cities at odd hours. He's even come to enjoy night traveling. It's less harried and the journey comes with time for quiet reflection. With the glowing ember of the cigarette arcing to his mouth again and again, Jeb leans back on a railing and reflects on why he's here.

He originally came to Boston to help organize dock workers. No success there. Little money. Little thanks. In need of funding and maybe a little adventure, he climbed aboard a late evening train to Cape Cod. It's a silly mission: find a rumored second survivor of the *Gossamer* shipwreck.

News of this alleged survivor came from Devlin Richards, the most troubling business partner Jeb has ever encountered. After their initial meeting, Jeb reached an uneasy peace with the man. But he knows Devlin will never fully trust someone who knows as much about him as Jeb now knows.

To maintain their truce, Jeb knows that he must find something during this trip—not just the sailor, but a real lead. A promise of riches.

Something.

Another cigarette burns. Inside the small station the conductor laughs and talks to another worker about the weather.

Bringing home "something" will be a challenge. Still, what Devlin was able to uncover, in just a few hours of poking around the port, was impressive. He gave Jeb enough of a lead to send him off to the Cape. A man with Devlin's skills could be an asset to someone

17

like Jeb. Devlin was willing to walk right into places where sane people fear to tread.

When Devlin turned up this lead, Jeb paid him his due, promised more money for more information, and climbed aboard the first train to Buzzards Bay.

Jeb walks to the end of the platform but can't see much of Quincy from where he stands. It looks like a nice enough town. Boston, on the other hand, had not been nice at all. At least not for Jeb.

New York, Chicago, the farm fields of Eastern Texas—all of those places had been fertile ground for the labor movement. Jeb could ride into most cities, find the angry workers (the poor slobs of the world), and he could easily mingle with them. He would make a few acquaintances, visit their wretched housing, quote Debs or Marx to them and find ways to get them working together in no time at all. The word "union" would start as a whisper. But angry men had a way of finding each other through those whispers. A cause was enjoined.

Striking together. Causing a scene. Making the newspapers. The process was always the same. A few concessions from the business owners would cool things down. Grateful workers would pay him a bit of money and he'd move on. He was slowly building a name for himself.

But Boston was much tougher, at least for Jeb. Labor was more entrenched and it had its own leaders and agenda. He hadn't expected that. One of the first unions in the country had been formed in Boston—the coopers and shoemakers. That was way back in the middle of the 1600s, for Christ's sake. So why wasn't Boston a more welcoming labor town for someone like him?

Jeb stubs out his butt and shakes his head. The Irish. That's the problem. They seem to be a whole union unto themselves. It never will be possible for him to work his way into that brotherhood. Same with the Italians. Italians in the North End of the city and Irish in the South. They keep the place locked down tight.

To survive these past weeks, Jeb had done a little shoplifting and snatched a wallet from a pocket or two. *Hard times*, he told himself. Just *hard times*. He's not really that sort of man.

The reason he had followed Rudolph Baines that night was not to rob and kill him like Devlin Richards, but to see where Baines lived. He wanted to rob the house, not the man.

Jeb sighs. He should have left Boston last week. Now he's found this wild goose and he's decided to chase it.

It's unfortunate that Devlin knows about the diamonds. But does he know, Jeb wonders, what else might have been on board the *Gossamer*? Before Devlin killed Baines, the merchant and his entourage had visited The Rose Point more than once. Jeb had been watching him. Learning about his dealings. Certain people, including Baines, were upset when the *Gossamer* departed a day early. They never had a chance to meet their connection.

They also discovered that the scientist on the ship, whoever he was, had become friends with the man who carried the diamonds. The two had been seen hovering around one of the big crates on the deck. Is that where he ended up hiding the stones? Was there any other value to the equipment in those crates?

One of the big boxes supposedly held only some wires and a tabletop generator. It wasn't that heavy. So if that crate floated free, then it had to be the one that was plucked from the sea—the one the sailor nailed his clothes to, poor bastard.

Finding that very crate was a long shot, but it was worth chasing. A crate full of scientific instruments that had been declared off limits to everyone else on the ship might indeed have been the perfect hiding place.

Jeb takes his time walking back up the platform. What would happen if he did become wealthy? Fun to think about. Would he retire, or would he use his wealth to continue his labor efforts?

Jeb knows the answer immediately. He'd carry on the fight. It's in his blood. And for that reason, Jeb will never view himself as a thief or a charlatan. He has an excuse. The street thievery. Trips like this one. All of it. The end justifies the means if you're helping the working man.

The conductor walks out of the building. Jeb rubs his eyes. They both climb back aboard, and the train groans out of the station, whistling into the night. They steam on, south and slightly east. Watching Quincy roll away. Watching the farm fields in the moonlight as they head toward the Cape. He really does like riding the night trains. This is his life for the time being.

Somewhere south of Quincy, at about 3:30 a.m., Jeb sees what looks like another train heading the opposite direction. Then he realizes there's not another set of tracks beside this one. It's just a road, a country lane with light-color dirt glowing in the moonlight.

He presses his face against the window, hands cupped around his eyes to see what's out there. What he spies is not one of those newfangled horseless carriages. Or if it is, it doesn't look anything like it should. A traction engine? A flaming carriage? Whatever the hell it is, it rushes past, hissing just like a steam engine. He pops open the window and thrusts his head out of the train car, just in time to see the bizarre vehicle disappear around a curve. It issues a series of clanks and rumbles that remind him of a hay wagon run amok. Atop it all, he sees long hair flapping in the wind behind a petite and crazed-looking driver.

Chapter 3

Industry

The lab assistant, the one they call Hans, stands in his white coat at the base of a large metal cylinder. The cylinder itself stands inside the Westinghouse research facility near Pittsburgh. Hans looks up at Nicola Tesla as the increasingly well-known scientist unbolts pieces of what looks like a giant birdcage at the cylinder's top.

"What do you mean you're leaving, Nikola? I don't understand. This work is important! How can you abandon what we're doing here?"

"I'm sorry, Hans." Nikola Tesla replies. "It's just time, that's all, time to go out on my own."

Hans shakes his head. "But why? We made such progress here, didn't we?" He watches with disdain as Tesla uses a rope to drop a set of iron braces to the floor. Climbing down, the Eastern European immigrant packs them in long wooden boxes.

Hans watches and his anger grows. To busy himself he starts sorting through other items, including tools and electrical parts. "After all that this company has done for you!" he mutters indignantly. "And all that George has done for you!"

Tesla looks annoyed. "You need to understand, Hans. I'm not leaving the company. Not exactly." He gives the younger man a box to hold, then dumps an armload of wires and switches into the container. "There. Put that with the rest of the stuff."

Hans continues to help, but his mood is somber. The older man realizes he must offer his friend and assistant a full explanation. "Look," Tesla growls in his Croatian accent, "George Westinghouse is talking about having me build a whole power plant for him. Can you believe it? A huge building, all dedicated to generating alternating current. We're talking about where to put it. It's possible that we might be able to locate it near Niagara Falls. Can you believe that? But at the same time he says the technology hasn't yet proven itself to the point where he wants to invest so much money. That means we need to conduct a big test or two first. We need something that's high profile. Something showy."

Hans' anger subsides, and he now looks interested. "What do you mean?"

"Do you know what's going on near Chicago right now? Construction. There are thousands of men out there building a sprawling complex. It's for a big gathering. A huge fair that will be held right outside of the city. It's supposed to open in a little more than a year, but from what I hear the whole thing has become so big that construction has fallen behind. It probably won't open until 1893."

"Yes. Yes, I've heard of that," Hans nods. "The Columbia Exhibition. I hope to visit there once it opens!"

"Well, guess what I have a chance to do, lad? I'm going to electrify that exhibition. The whole damn fair. First time electric lights will be installed in such a size and scope. And we're not just going to string lights. We're going to integrate electricity into everything. You won't even see the wires—they'll be buried. And you won't just see bare bulbs like you do around here. They're planning to design beautiful street lamps and hanging fixtures. They'll be just like the fanciest gas lamps you ever saw."

"Alternating current or direct?" Hans asks with fascination.

Tesla smiles. "It will all be driven by alternating current. This fair, this Columbia Exhibition near Chicago, will be my proving ground. Do you understand now why this is so important Hans? See why I have to put our other experiments away for a while?"

Hans nods. "Of course I understand. It's a very big opportunity for you, Nikola. Very big indeed."

"Once I get things set up, maybe I'll send for you. I'll need skilled engineers."

The younger man grins with pride. "Yes. Please do. I'd be proud to be part of that!"

Tesla draws an arc in the air with both hands. "Wait until you see it. We will show the world what electricity can really do. They'll realize it's not just about lights anymore. That's just the start. We're planning an elevated electric railway. Can you imagine that?" Tesla's hands wave wildly in the air. "And they're going to test electric boats in the canals. They're even talking about building a moving electric sidewalk! Can you picture such a thing? Can we even build it? It will be wondrous. Miraculous! It's a glimpse of what the future will hold! Hans … can you imagine… people are going to be shocked when they see all the things our alternating current can do."

"Yes, Yes!" Hans laughs. "Take me with you now then! Invite Raymond too! You said they have thousands of workers already. They must need more!"

"No, no … I'm not ready for the electrical workers yet. They won't be installing the generators for months. We're still doing the planning. I don't even have to be in Chicago for that, so I'm taking a leave of absence for a few months. I'm moving to New York. I have over thirty inventions that I'm trying to patent, but I keep getting distracted here. I have paperwork spread everywhere."

Tesla stares toward the small windows at the far end of the room. "So many details. So much to do. So many ideas. Sometimes I just…"

Hans waits for a few moments, then adds, "I hear the Chicago Fair will be even bigger than the Centennial Exhibition in Philadelphia."

"Well, of course," Tesla responds. "This is a bigger country now, no? You and I, Hans, neither of us were here fifteen years ago. We are newcomers since then, eh? There are hundreds of thousands more like us. Newcomers. Look how America grows."

"Yes, it does indeed," Hans says with a smile.

"When I talked to George Westinghouse about doing this work, we also talked about how frightening all the changes have been for people. Look what people are learning to use today! Lights. Telephones. And soon there will be many more automobiles. Think of how that will scare people who don't understand the march of technology."

Hans considers this. "But why do they fear such changes? Shouldn't they instead admire these things and take pride in their country's accomplishments? Shouldn't the progress make them proud?"

"Bah. You would think so, wouldn't you? But people can be stupid. They fear what they don't know." Tesla points toward a stack of notebooks. "But I have other things to worry about. I have to clean up this mess first, Hans. I know you think we can make money from radio if we ever perfect it. But how much money am I missing out on already by not finishing these patent applications?"

Tesla finishes packing his experiments and nails down the tops of the boxes.

"So where does that leave us then?" Hans asks. "Where does it leave this work?"

"It leaves it stalled for a while, Hans. Just on hold. I'm sorry." He looks his friend in the eyes. "Ever since we lost Victor and his equipment in that storm, it's been tough for me to focus on radio. But you have other duties here, and I have my work to do far away from here. Let us busy ourselves with other things. When it's time to install the generators at the exhibition, I will send for you. I'd be proud to work with you and Raymond again. Just understand that it may be several months."

Hans shakes his head. "It's like you're pushing our radio research out of your mind, along with Victor."

Tesla sighs.

They haul the boxes out to a waiting wagon. Hans helps lift them up as Tesla stacks them neatly in the bed. From the wagon they can see out across a large wheat field. At the far side a farmer walks behind a plow pulled by an ox.

"You see that man over there, Hans? That's still the largest industry in this country. Agriculture. Family farms. That's the kind of work that's still the foundation of America. But you and I, we see the change coming. Think of what we're going to build in Chicago next year. The engines. The walkways. So many lights. It will show everyone the power of the electric industry, lad. New kinds of machines will let us do so much. Trust me. The average person in this country isn't going to be a farmer for much longer."

After they tie the load into place, Tesla climbs up into the seat. Hans shakes his hand and bids him well.

"I've enjoyed working with you, sir. I've learned a lot."

"We'll work together again. Be sure of it."

"But will we continue our radio experiments some day? Or can I expect to just work on generators from now on?"

"Of course we'll continue. When I'm set up in New York, I plan to dedicate one room just to radio testing. I'm sure I'll be able to make some more discoveries."

"No you won't. You won't have enough room if you're in a place like New York."   ·

Tesla laughs. "Don't be so sure. Remember our last experiment? When we almost killed that photographer? I realized right then that it's not just a matter of making bigger sparks to make bigger radio waves. We were going down the wrong path with those tests. When Victor was still with us he agreed to test some of these theories, and I believe he was heading down the correct path. The power has to be applied in a very specific way. I have some sketches that my old friend sent to me, and I have some new ideas of my own. Yes, we'll keep going, Hans, and we won't need a room the size of a barn to do it."

"I'm going to miss your silly accent around here," Hans calls out as the horse cart pulls away. "But I'm not going to miss that droopy mustache!"

Tesla just laughs and drives away from the Westinghouse complex – up the road to the east. Hans heads back into the building, hands thrust into the pockets of his coat. It's starting to dawn on him how empty the building feels and how dull his work is going to seem now that the outrageous and ingenious Nikola Tesla has moved on.

Chapter 4

Remembrance

Amanda's former neighborhood sits on a small hill at the far quadrant of Boston's North End. From the street level she can see the white steeple of the Old North Church.

One if by land. Two if by sea.

Early settlers here were English, then the Irish. Now the neighborhood holds a growing number of Italian families. The city's newest immigrants are attracted by the cheaper prices of the older houses. In front of those houses drifts the scent of red sauce, garlic, and boiled pasta. Cooking is an all-day affair for the Italian women. Heavyset housewives visit each other's homes. They sample what's simmering on the stoves and loudly argue about textures, spices, and ways to serve their concoctions.

Amanda pays attention to ethnic eccentricities because she herself is the product of what stuffily proper people in Boston would consider a mixed marriage. Her father was an Italian stone mason who came to America before the current influx of Italian workers. Her mother was thin, pale, freckled, and very Irish. Her mother tried to steer Amanda toward the other Irish children as playmates, but Amanda preferred to play with anyone who seemed adventurous, no matter where their parents were from.

Now, as she walked the North End streets, she could see just how unusual her life was. The Italian mothers all stand together. Talk together. Cook together. Their children play together.

The Irish mothers stand in their own small groups, hushed whispers growing even softer if a stranger walks past.

27

Stranger. Yes, that's what she is now. If only her gaze could settle upon a familiar face.

She continues her walk north. Smaller row houses here, many in need of paint. Finally she nears the street where she grew up. Tears form in her eyes, but she blinks and wills them away. At street level, it's mostly dark stone steps and coal-dust stained sidewalks. Upper floors have moss growing in cracks while many of the basement windows are broken and patched with cardboard.

It's been nearly three years since she's visited this street and well over a year since she received a letter from an old neighbor, and that neighbor was in the process of moving. That was the last person she knew from the old neighborhood.

Amanda doesn't feel safe here anymore. Two of the houses mid-street are empty. Gutted by fire. Doors are missing. Rough-looking men sit on those stoops. Squatters.

Across the street someone stares out through cracked glass. She decides to move on. A few more steps and she sees the apartment she called home during her teen years, right after her father died. It looks occupied still, but quite disheveled. An eclectic mix of ethnicities sit on the front stoop, eyes tracking her.

"Does Martha Raines still live here?" Amanda asks the group.

"Who?" a dark-skinned teenage girl asks.

"Martha Raines. Apartment 2B. She lived here for years."

Someone laughs.

"Ain't nobody in 2B now 'cept that old man. Been here maybe six months."

Amanda looks down.

"He don't talk to nobody. We don't talk to him much neither."

One of the men in the group, thin and with a hefty cough, sits up straight. "Why you asking, Miss? Why you looking for this Raines lady?"

"She ... well, she was just a friend. That's all."

"You might look over on Platt Street. Couple people from this building moved over there. That's all I know."

And that was the end of it. Martha was one of the few people who Amanda thought might still be living in the old building. She'd hoped that she could reconnect with her and, with her help, contact others she used to know. Maybe even move back here. But from the looks of it, this isn't even a place she wants to visit again.

Amanda walks halfheartedly to Platt Street but finds nothing. No familiar faces and no Martha. Eventually she takes a streetcar to the home of Sadie, an old friend of her mother's. Amanda knocks twice before the woman answers, bony knuckles grasping the handle. It takes the old woman a few moments to recognize Amanda, but when she does, she offers a great hug and invites her inside. Sadie brushes her apron. Loose flour falls on the doorstep.

This is more like it, Amanda thinks as she walks through the front hallway. The parlor has bright freshly painted walls and a yellow and red rug. Plants dot the edges of the tall bay window.

They sit in the kitchen and talk for some time. Amanda smiles as she hears a few familiar names. She learns who has moved, who's married now and who has died. All of this news tells Amanda there will be no easy re-entry to her old life. The friends of her youth all have married and moved elsewhere. There are no great job prospects nearby, and no easy "friend of a friend" connections to exploit.

"Have you thought of moving to someplace like Lowell and working as a mill girl?" Sadie asks. "I'm not sure if they're hiring as many new girls as they were a few years back."

"No. I haven't thought about that. Not sure yet if I want to leave Boston again."

"Well, let's see. My nephew used to work in a bakery about two blocks from here," Sadie says, "but he joined the army about six months ago."

"Do you know the manager there? Could I mention your nephew's name?"

Sadie grows quiet. "Well, dear, I don't think that would be wise. Let's just say that he didn't part with that place on the best of terms. In fact, I think that's one of the reasons he ran off to join the army."

Another cup of tea and eventually Amanda says good-bye, with a painfully short list of names of people who may know of employment opportunities. She also carries a small tin of cookies and she promises to come back for Sunday dinner sometime soon. She notices, as she reaches the bottom of the front stoop, that her lip has grown sore. That's when she realizes how often she'd chewed on it today.

With nowhere else to go, she returns to the Morgans', walking all the way to save the streetcar fare.

She helps Beverly prepare dinner and confesses that her job prospects are dim. As if apologizing, Amanda then shows Beverly the list of prospects she's collected and says she'll visit each of them in the morning.

"Dear, please, don't worry about that. We'll help you until you get on your feet. And maybe I can come up with an idea or two for you."

A pot roast sits in the wood-fired oven. Beverly walks through the back alley, stopping at several neighbors' houses. She eventually returns with the name of a shopkeeper who may be looking for a girl to help keep his books. He's out of town now but will return a week from Tuesday. Feeling a bit better, Amanda shoos Beverly out of her own kitchen.

"The least I can do is serve you dinner since you've been so nice to me."

She searches for the best dishes she can find without tapping into the family's good china. Then she carries everything to the table, pours water for the three of them, and finally sits down, linen napkin in her lap.

She brushes aside their thanks by saying, "Nonsense, it's the least I can do. I'll cook a few times each week if you let me." She also promises to pay them for her room and board as soon as she is able.

Beverly helps clear the table, in spite of Amanda's protests. Together, they wash and dry the dishes, then carry the glassware back to a fat doily-covered sideboard in the dining room.

It's too early to retire. Amanda wonders if she should spend the late afternoon chasing down some of the job leads on her list. But before going out, she has to clear up an issue that's troubling her.

"Excuse me, Beverly," she says, folding a dishrag neatly on the edge of the porcelain sink and taking a deep breath. "Do you mind if I ask you something?"

Chapter 5

Inquiry

Devlin Richards sits at the northern edge of Boston Common and looks toward a distant clock tower. It's nine in the morning. A light fog burns off and tries to drift in the general direction of the ocean.

In the short period of time he's been in Boston, he's learned that the northern end is the quieter end of this park, at least in the morning. That's good. Fewer passersby will overhear his conversation. He only waits a few minutes before he spots a police officer. Right on time. This should be Officer Hudson, his contact and unofficial "in" at the Boston Police Department. The man in blue wanders up from the south and takes a seat on the same bench.

Devlin has been keeping the name of this officer in his back pocket for some time. It was given to him when he was traveling by mail boat, up the coast from South Carolina. Until now he had actively avoided police contact. But a thought had occurred to him a few days ago. With a little luck, he might be able to turn his Boston visit into an important side project. The fact that his life in Charleston South Carolina fell apart has a direct connection to this city and this state. As long as he's here, maybe he can do something about that.

"You're the one who wanted this meeting," the patrolman says gruffly. "Start talking."

Devlin nods. "Do you know where I got your name?"

"Yes, I know. Captain of the postal boat. He sent me a note saying you might be in contact. I'd about given up that I'd ever hear from you."

"Does he send you a lot of contacts?"

Hudson scoffs. "Only the ones with some sort of problem attached to them. I'm guessing that's you, eh? Weighing in with some sort of problem? Lucky me."

Devlin nods again.

"Am I supposed to hear the coins rattle in your head? Or do you have some sort of business proposition you want to make Southern boy?"

Devlin bites is tongue. Takes a breath. "You do prefer to get right to the point, don't you?"

The patrolman scoffs again. "You see this park? I walk it every day. When some problem crops up, I'm glad to handle it. I'm good that way. No one does jack-all around here without having to answer to the law and to me. But it's not about always being the good guy. Sometimes it's about being the guy who does favors. I think you know that, right? I think so because you were given my name for a reason. I don't know what that reason is, yet. So if you want to talk business? Start talking."

The pause is long. Hudson starts to stand, but Devlin makes a motion with his hand. "Hang on. Just trying to think of the best way to explain this."

"Ain't got all day boy."

Devlin's mood changes. "That's the second time you've called me boy. Call me boy again and we won't be doing business," Devlin looks him deep in the eye. "Or maybe our business will change to something completely different."

"That a fact?"

They stare each other down for a moment,

"Still waiting for that story…"

Devlin nods slowly, and starts to share his tale.

"I'm looking for two men. One by the name of Peter Jacobs. The other's called Earl Lindley. I have business with one of them. But I'll take either."

"Don't know either of those names. Should I?"

"Not necessarily. Just wondering if you can help find one or both of them."

The cop shrugs. "For the right reason, I might be able to look. You have the right reason for me?"

"I have several coins in my pocket. At least one is gold. The others are silver."

Hudson nods. "Gold I might be interested in. Doesn't sound like a whole lot at stake though. Just one coin."

Devlin brushes some dust off his pants. He lets the moment linger. "I'm asking for information. Nothing more dangerous than that. Gold is a decent payday for a little info."

"What's the background? This man a criminal? Wronged you? If so, even a damn secesh like you could walk into any police station and swear out a complaint. You don't need me to be involved."

Devlin grits his teeth. "As far as I'm concerned, you federal, he is very much a criminal. But others might not necessarily agree with me, and that's what brought me here. To you."

Officer Hudson closes his eyes. "Christ, you fucking old rebel. Is this some sort of carpetbagger vendetta? It is, isn't it? We used to get those on occasion. Not for a long time though. I know the whole story. Bastards came down there, stole from you, and hightailed it back up north. But it's been, what? Twenty five years? "

"Twenty six."

"Well, the country has long since moved on. Just accept it."

"It's…" The southerner wonders just how much to tell. He decides to lay his cards on the table. "It's only vaguely a vendetta against a thief. There's much more to the story. But, yes, there's a bit of an eye-for-an-eye aspect to what I'm seeking. I'll admit that."

"Hey!" Officer Hudson shouts suddenly. But the exclamation isn't directed at Devlin. A disheveled man walks across the grass near them. He's obviously drunk, despite the early hour, and he's picking at bottles and bits of litter to see what he can find.

"Hang on a moment," Hudson holds a finger up to Devlin.

"You! Stop there! What the hell are you doing?"

The bum looks startled. "I don't know. Looking?"

"Get out of my park," Hudson commands.

"What? I, I mean, I just…" The words are slurred, but it's obvious the poor bastard is ready to argue for his right to walk across the park.

"None of your damn lip! I'm here to keep things safe, and that means I don't need shits like you pawing through the trash and pissing in the bushes." He stands, walks over to the bum and kicks him in the ass. The man stumbles, recovers and runs toward the edge of the park.

"Don't let me see your sorry face in my park again," Hudson calls after him, "unless you're shaved, showered and you're only walking across my grass because you're on your way to work."

35

Devlin starts to mutter something about that being typical Yankee overreaction, but bites his tongue.

"You were saying? Something about an eye for an eye, wasn't it?"

Devlin squints. "Okay. I'll be frank. And I'll try to tell you the whole story." He takes a deep breath and begins. "It was February, 1865. The war wasn't over yet, but it was damn sure headed that way. The 55th regiment, bunch of Massachusetts boys, came through my town. We'd been beaten down pretty hard by then. I'm not saying there wasn't still a good bit of southern resistance here and there, but it was more pride and resentment lashing on, not any real fighting."

"Yeah. I remember Charleston's end," Hudson responds. "It was in the papers here. My dad and uncles talked about it. I was 14 at the time. Was thinking about signing up just so I'd be there to see the last of it. But they wouldn't let me. After dropping the age limit for enlistments for three years, they started raising it again. Suddenly 14 was too young. Made me pretty mad. I never got to go south.

"Well, be glad of it. Doesn't matter if you get killed in the opening salvo of a war, or in the final days. You're still dead."

Hudson shakes his head. "Just finish your story, hey?"

Devlin takes a nods and starts again.

"You were 14? I was 17 at the time. Been fighting since 15. I was about done with it by the end, I can tell you. I was in the South Carolina 10th Infantry Regiment. Fought in a series of skirmishes in Mississippi, Kentucky and eventually Tennessee. Things got bogged down at the rivers, so some of us broke off and joined another unit that was heading north to meet the Yank's head on. But then things went bad. It became obvious we were just cannon fodder rushing toward those relentless fucks in blue. We had no real strategy or guidance. I took a bullet in the back, and luckily it passed on through, only nicking a few places. But that bullet was my ticket to a hospital, and then my ticket back home. But it came at the wrong time."

"So back home wasn't safe?"

"No, back home is where everything went to shit. I was there recuperating, walking around a bit with a cane, when the 55th came to call. I don't know if you know anything about that unit, but them soldiers were niggers. Least the enlisted boys were. Massachusetts had its more well-known 54th Regiment with its black faces. Right? You ever hear of them?

Hudson gives a half shrug. "They were from around here. So, yes. But most of us didn't really learn about them until after the war."

"Yeah, well, the 55th was sort of a spill-over from that regiment. Late-comers to the army plus some other niggers who came from other states. Looking to join the festivities, I guess. Well, when the 55th entered Charleston, you should have seen the reception. Every house or field servant who could get away ran to line the streets once they heard that there was black union soldiers marching in. Standing three deep most places. They were woopin' and hollerin' and cussin'. A fine how-do-you-do, I'll tell ya. And then those boys, those niggers in blue, they started singing as they were marching. Hymns at first. Then some tunes that only they seemed to know. That was something to see, all right. I just bit my tongue and wandered back home."

"What was your business there, before the war? Or... your family's business."

Devlin manages to steer the conversation in a new direction, never quite answering the question.

37

"Anyway, I had been back at my house for about an hour, when the boys came marching right up Kings Road. They took a left at the square and they walked right up to the front door of our house. Nicest house on the block, so that might have had something to do with their visit. It wasn't just the enlisted men though. They had white Yankees with them by that time. Officers. They banged hard. Chipped the front door. One of them produced an iron pry bar, so we decided to just open the door. The white men, the officers, came in."

" 'We' opened the door? Who is we?"

"My sister, my mother, and I."

"Why was your house the nicest on the block? I don't think you answered the question about what you did."

"Import export business," Devlin says, "Shipping. Related to the textile trade." He's surprised when the vague answer is enough to satisfy Hudson. "There was five of the white officers. They came in and at first they asked a lot of questions. Said they were looking for any hiding rebel soldiers. But three of them stayed with us in the parlor, as the other two disappeared into the house. We could hear them searching and moving things around."

"Any trap doors here?" one of them asked. "I'll bust your nose if we find one and you haven't told me."

"'Nothing for you here,' my sister said, 'we're done. All of us. Done to death.'"

Devlin takes a long breath in. "The sounds coming from the other room started to sound less like searching, and more like taking. Or, more like quiet, outright stealing. Items being lifted from shelves. Silverware drawers being opened and emptied. I wasn't expecting that kind of thing from officers. But they were young, and battle

38

hardened. I stood up to intervene and got a rifle butt in the middle of my back."

"So they took your stuff? Okay. It was war. Things happen. Yankees ain't any more honest than you rebels when it comes right down to it."

"Took? Yes. They took alright,"

"So. Those two names you mentioned. How do you actually know those names?"

"They were sloppy. Barely professional soldiers. I heard first names a few times. Then last names as they called to each other from room to room. It wasn't too hard to figure out who was who. "

"You got the name of just two of them?"

"I actually got the name of four of them. And there was a time when I wanted to get my revenge on each. But time dampens harsh feelings. As a solider in grey, I certainly helped myself a few times when we were looking in houses. I know the temptation. So I couldn't be too strict about it, despite the personal violation. War is war."

"Noble of you. I guess. So why just those two?"

"Because those two grabbed my sister, pushed her outside, and dragged her into a root cellar. I jumped to stop them, and got another rifle butt, this one in the cheek. My lights went out for a bit. Two went upstairs to rummage there. The other soldier stayed in the kitchen, pointing a gun at me and my mother. We heard her screams. Begged him to go stop his friends. But he laughed. "This is about taking, rebel scum. Get used to it," I was dizzy but I do remember those words, even though my chest hurt, my cheek hurt and the whole room seemed foggy. Her screaming stopped. It sounded like the two men were switching places. Took her again, they did. More screams, I tried to rise, but got the final knee right to my nose and forehead. Lights out.

Devlin pauses for a long time. "According to my mother, God rest her soul, they switched places twice. Eventually one of the other soldiers came down from the upstairs and looked guilty. He moved to break things up and swore at the raping bastards, but they just laughed. He didn't have the gumption to do any more than just scold them and chase them back to the ranks.

"I didn't wake up until the following morning, but those names were burned in my head. They came from Massachusetts. That's all I know. I'm in town on business. Figured I'd start here."

Hudson snorts. "So that's what this is all about? Sounds like a fool's errand to me."

"Maybe it is. But as long as I'm here, it seems appropriate to try to look them up."

"I see," the officer replies. "And why are you here exactly? Besides the revenge thing."

"Like I said. Business."

The pair sit in silence for several minute. Another disheveled man walks by, but Hudson takes no notice. Finally he says. "I got a sister myself you know. Man's got a right to protect his kin. We both know that. Time's passed though. Way too much time."

"It ain't for me,"

Hudson hesitates. "So, let's say one of these guys does live here in the city. And that alone is a long-shot. And let's say I help you track one or both of them down, because of your offer of gold coins – and notice I said coins, plural, not just the one in your pocket. What's your plan? I don't need any new bodies piling up."

"Assuming you can find one, I think I'll just have a little chat with him. I think an apology might be in order, and maybe he can provide a nice letter of apology to my sister."

"Bullshit."

Devlin laughs harder than he has since arriving in Boston.

"Look if you find him, and if you want to go there and deliver some message, that's fine. But I'm supposed to be a peace keeper. If things get too rough, I'll track you down again too. Believe me. I don't want to see any bodies. Got it?

Devlin smiles. "If you don't find any leads, we may never need to talk again, officer. But I hope we do. If you need to reach me, please leave a message with the bartender at the Rose Point. I've been visiting there a few times each week. It's quite an interesting establishment."

Chapter 6

Suspicion

The land mass of Cape Cod is often compared to a giant curled arm that reaches out to sea, like a man flexing his muscle. If that's the case, then Buzzards Bay is nestled in the Cape's armpit.

But that's a circumstance of geography, not an insult. The area itself is wildly beautiful. Approaching Buzzards Bay by train is like riding along the rim of a great green saucer. There are no large hills nor valleys in this thrust of land. There's just a long, shallow slope that eventually merges with the sea. The train skirts the edge of this slope, along the perimeter of a small forest. As it puffs through the final few miles, the train's windows offer a spectacular view of the water. Then the rails curve away from the shoreline, leading toward a small village.

Jeb Thomas has ridden these last few miles in wonder. What he sees out the early morning train window is a mix of the traditional and the strangely exotic.

The edges of Cape Cod have the same look as the rest of New England. There are tidy colonial houses, white churches, and winding dirt roads. But it's different too. There are fewer stones walls here. The soil takes on a whitish look. The trees are a bit shorter and scrubbier. Even the birds are more alien to him—similar, yet not quite the same as what he's seen near Boston. Everything seems to have a subtle variance, from the size of the houses to the look of the roads. Taken en masse, all of these differences announce that he has arrived in a wilder, stranger outpost of the New England tradition.

This is also an ancient place, at least by American standards. Jeb has traveled the country enough to know that 250-year-old houses are a rare thing in the United States. How many white people lived in this land in the 1630s? Jeb has no idea, but those people certainly weren't building houses in Chicago or St. Louis. Yet here, in the coastal areas of southern Massachusetts, the landscape is dotted with those early homes. Dates are printed with pride on plaques attached to the sides of houses. *Circa 1639. Circa 1697.* Along with Virginia, this area marked the dawn of one civilization and the long slow demise of another.

Jeb leans back in the seat and feels the rumble of the steel wheels.

White people. Oldest houses and buildings in the country, is that what they think they have? Jeb has seen the nation's oldest buildings, and they sure as hell aren't located in New England or Virginia.

Three years prior he had visited El Paso. He was chased away from a Texas migrant labor meeting by the local sheriff, and he found refuge in an aged Catholic mission called Ysleta del Sur. Over a meager dinner of bread and beans, a priest there told him that parts of the mission had been built in the early 1500s. Imagine that. America, actually had buildings that were nearly 400 years old. And what about the adobe structures he's seen from the trains as he crossed the desert? Even older than that. Some of those adobes were a thousand years old, if not more.

Seeing these white clapboard cape houses, Jeb mutters to himself that it's not who came first that matters in the long run; it's really about winning the cultural battle and having more people. What was built here is what became the nation's dominant archetype, and that's why this coastline seems like America's cradle.

Jeb's grandfather traveled from Aberdeen, Scotland, to Boston sixty years before and settled somewhere south of the city. Dedham? Was that the name of the town? Jeb's father, Fletcher Thomas, had been the restless one. With no interest in farming or learning a trade, he had left the family home in Dedham and moved to central New York, where he took a bride. Then they moved to Ohio. Then beyond. Every five years or so Fletcher Thomas found a new outlook for himself and headed to a new city.

Jeb's dad was a railroad worker for a while. Then he worked in a textile mill. Then he worked in a factory that made guns. Then it was back to the railroad again and on to more factories. Growing up, Jeb had learned three things from his father. The first was a love of travel and adventure. The second was a respect for business mixed with a disrespect for factory and railroad owners who didn't take care of their workers. The third was a lingering anxiety from the constant moving. The beckoning horizon held romance and adventure for his dad, but for a young boy with few friends, moving also was something to be feared. Jeb saw his mother close slowly inward, with no permanent set of friends to sustain her. He eventually saw his father, robust and audacious in his youth, evolve into an old man with no real community around him, and no lasting legacy.

Yet, Jeb overcame his childhood fear of travel and focused instead on his fascination with what might lay beyond the horizon.

Fighting for the working man actually gave him an excuse to travel and to learn. But he vowed to himself he would never marry and start a family until he someday finds the place where he wants to stay for good. Maybe as a local union representative at some factory successful enough to pay a decent wage.

The train starts to slow. They must be nearing Falmouth. There are more white houses here and occasional small shops. But he sees nothing resembling a factory.

The conductor makes his final pass through the car. He nods to Jeb.

"How's it coming along?" Jeb asks. The conductor scans the length of the car before answering. No one seems to be listening.

"The group, you mean? I guess it's coming." The conductor knows Jeb only because another conductor made arrangements for Jeb to travel for free this evening. He knows only that Jeb has something to do with their union. "Why? What do you know about it?"

"Not much. Edward, do you know Edward? He told me that you were all trying to unionize. He thought I might be able to help. That's what I do, though I don't know much about his plans yet."

The conductor leans against the wooden armrest of a seat across from Jeb.

"Well, we've had four meetings already. There's only about eight of us. We probably need more than that if this thing's going to happen."

Jeb nods. "How many conductors total?"

"On this line? Only eighteen. We're a small company."

"Think you can get twelve of them?"

"Maybe. I'm thinking we can. Men are all fed up. This line's making good money and we're not seeing any of it."

Jeb nods and hands him a union pin. It has "Switchmen's Mutual Aid Association" printed on yellow tin with a wreath of leaves along the outer edge and a stylized "S" in the middle.

"Now, I wouldn't wear that just yet," Jeb says, "but it's a good thing to keep in your pocket. Show it to the others if they seem interested. Show them they can be part of something much larger if they all work together."

"You a member of that union?"

"I'm a member of all unions. One big union, that's what I see."

The conductor looks at the logo. "Switchmen, hum? What's that got to do with conductors like me?"

"Union's a union. The bigger the better. You get more clout."

"Yeah, but why would they want conductors in their brotherhood?"

"Like I said. Safety in numbers. Look at me. My friends take care of me. That's why you never asked me for my ticket on this whole ride. See?"

The conductor smirks.

Jeb laughs out loud. "I'm like a ghost who passes through, right? You know that. Union men, we look out for each other."

The conductor slips the pin into his pocket. "Fair enough. I might just hang onto this. Switchmen's union's out of Chicago, right?"

Jeb nods. "Ayah, started there. Grown considerably in the past fourteen years." Wherever he goes, Jeb does his best to talk the local talk. He's not entirely sure if *ayah* is an expression more appropriate to southern or northern New England, but he works it in.

"Yeah," the conductor continues, "Switchmen's Mutual was growing right good until about three years ago, right? Big old strike against the Chicago, Burlington, and Quincy line. Men got locked out. Long damn time as I recollect. Some of the men just left, got jobs elsewhere. Those that stuck it out eventually went back with their

46

hats in hands. Didn't get a damn thing 'cept a lot of pain." He lets his words settle in. "Am I right?"

"As you tell it, I guess you are. Every brotherhood has its ups and downs."

"Umm hum." The conductor takes the pin back out of his pocket and flips the button in the air a few times, like a coin with heads but no tails. "That why you're here, mister? I'd think any man who helped build a switchman's union would have better things to do than recruit on a small potatoes line like this one." He looks Jeb in the eye. "'Cept maybe you don't, eh? I imaging that if you lose a big one like that, then it gets a bit tougher to do the next labor action. And then the next one too. Sense of trust is gone, hum? Other players emerge?"

He hands the pin back to Jeb.

"Changed my mind. I appreciate the offer, mister, but our little group is also talking with the Order of Railway Conductors of America. If we do unionize, fairly sure that's who we'll go with. Not the Switchmen."

Jeb nods. "All right. But I have connections to far bigger groups. Just so you know."

"We ain't like the engineers or the switchmen. If we walk off, we ain't going to stop the trains. They'll just fire our asses and bring in more of the coloreds. Already said they might do that anyway. Them coloreds work cheap."

"I know. It's happening all over."

Jeb sighs as the conductor leaves. It's best that he doesn't mention that he's also helped to organize groups of negroes in the South. In fact, the black conductor groups are becoming powerful enough, and willing to work cheaply enough, that they'll likely take

47

over most of the conductor slots on the main rail lines within ten years.

Jeb pulls his small pack out from under the seat. The conductor's words had stung him. He had indeed been a rising star in the labor movement, but now he feels stalled. He's living on dimes, promises and occasional kindness from small groups. Maybe it really is time to pass this torch to someone else. Maybe it's time to settle down, find that perfect small town with a big factory. Let someone else fight the bigger fights.

He remembers one more thing about that night at Ysleta del Sur. That priest, in his mix of Spanish and broken English, had insisted Jeb would be more effective in his work if he became part of the priesthood. "From one brotherhood to another," the priest had joked, "I'd like to remind you that the *brotherhood of the Father*," he pointed up, "is always recruiting."

Jeb tried to laugh it off.

"I'm quite serious, amigo," Father Diego said. "We have a special appreciation for men who carry with them a moral commitment to help others. That is you, no?"

"You sure that's not just the wine going to your head padré?"

"No. Not at all, my friend. I do believe what I say here. If you centered your organization skills on spirituality as much as you do on business and politics, then it might actually be easier for you to gain the trust of the workers. They are good people. Devout people, though poor, most of them. They want to know that you are a good person too. I'm tired of seeing poor people struggle, and I do think some unions, in some cases, might help them."

Jeb said nothing, but he rejected the whole idea. Of all the organizations he'd ever seen, none offered a stranger mix of both support and oppression than organized religion. He, more than anyone, realized that brotherhoods could be a double-edged sword. But he was more than happy to hide in this ancient church and share the wine, nodding as the priest's voice echoed off the stone walls built by a failed Spanish empire.

He looks out the train window again and sees a quaint white house, two stories, precise overlapping clapboards, front door in the dead center, windows all exactly the same size and perfectly spaced. This simple house could be the very model for similar ones all over America. New England as a gateway. History written by the winners and printed on the collective memory.

It's well past daybreak when they pull into Falmouth. No wagon drivers or cabs lurk near the tiny station. Downtown isn't far away, and the walk takes him past white picket fences and once-neat lawns burned brown by the summer sun. Rounding a corner, he follows a horse-drawn wagon with a large water tank mounted in the back. A T-shaped bar sticks down, and a fine mist of oily water sprays out onto the street, dampening the dusty road. Every few minutes the wagon driver reaches back to grasp a handle, pumping air into the top of the tank. Two dogs run along behind, darting in and out of the mist and biting at the streams.

Only one business is open when Jeb reaches the village center, a small restaurant at the far end of a line of storefronts. All heads turn to look as he enters. Then they look away. Falmouth may be a small town, but it's also a place that a lot of people pass through, especially if you're heading out to the islands of Martha's Vineyard or Nantucket.

Jeb thinks about those islands as he takes a seat. Whalers. What a challenge it would be to try to unionize that rowdy lot. Tough, crazy, and tattooed, is there any group that needs organization more than a gang of sailors who risks their lives while reaping such small rewards for themselves? But he knows it's a silly thought. The golden age of whaling has passed. It would be a waste of his time.

With a nice tip to the waitress for his cup of coffee, he asks the whereabouts of the town doctor and is given detailed directions to his house. In fifteen minutes he's there, finding a plump, middle-aged woman seated at a roll-top desk just inside the door.

She smiles slightly, but casts a wary eye over him. He's not there for treatment, and she can tell.

"Lovely day, isn't it, ma'am?"

She nods and stares back.

"I'm … um … looking for a friend of mine. A sailor. I understand he was treated here a few days ago. Wrecked on the *Gossamer*. Lucky to be alive. I'm hoping to catch up with him. Wish him well."

"And why are you asking me?"

"Well, I … um … was hoping you could help me find him. After all, he is recovering in town, isn't he?"

She pulls her glasses down slightly and looks over them. "The doctor prefers that we don't give out information on any of our patients."

Jeb leans against the door casing, smiling. Giving her his look, the one that says he is sweet, innocent, friendly. The kind of guy she should trust.

He changes his tactic slightly. Acts like a man she could laugh with and maybe enjoy.

"I know. And that's very admirable. Privacy in medical matters is so important." She isn't biting, and he can see that he's losing her.

The charm just doesn't seem to turn on all the way. Perhaps he's too tired.

"Look. I just want to say hi to him. See that he's okay. Could you ask the doctor if that's a good idea? If he's not up to it, I certainly don't want to bother the poor guy. But if he's strong enough, then, you know, seeing a friend might help him feel a little better. That's all."

She looks at him, indifferent.

"Fine. I understand. If I can't help him, then I can't." He turns to leave, knowing there are several other avenues to pursue in a small town.

The woman sits still for several seconds then slowly rises, making her way toward the back of the large house that serves as the doctor's office. Jeb hears hushed tones in a far room, then something that sounded like, "Well, I don't know, but if you say so, doctor."

Finally the woman returns, looking a bit miffed.

"The doctor can't see you right now. He's preparing to go deliver a baby. But he says your friend's fever finally broke last night and that he's had a good night's rest. It might be okay for you to stop in later today."

"Excellent! Stop in where?"

She hesitates. "Well, there's an inn near the square. He's staying upstairs there."

Jeb nods.

"Gray building. Dark shutters," she adds.

"I do thank you. It will be nice to catch up with him."

"So how do you know him?" she asks.

"Oh, um … we went to school together, years ago."

"Where was that?"
"Um … in Boston."

"Strange, I thought he was from down south somewhere."

"Oh—yes, yes, he was, but this was a sailing school. You know, not really a school. Just a bunch of guys learning about knots and stuff and an old sailor who was teaching us. It was hard to get work on the ships a few years ago if you didn't have experience, so some of the old sailors picked up a bit of drinking money by teaching groups like ours."

Jeb thought hard of a way to change the subject. "So hey … that was some way they found him, eh? All nailed to the crate like that. Pretty resourceful, I'd say."

"Oh, yes. I heard about that. But he must have felt so terrible, drifting along like that."

They both nod, then laugh uneasily. "Say, where did they bring him in?"

"Right into the harbor off Scranton Avenue."

"Well, I hope someone saved that crate for him. It would be quite a souvenir, I should think. Not often a man gets to save his life using something like that."

"Oh, I think they did. Someone hauled it over to the Andrews cold storage building. It's a big icehouse where they store food and beer. I heard they put it in the back area."

"Good. Good. I can't wait to hear the story from him."

That was what he needed. If he can find that crate Jeb might not even have to visit the sailor. He bids the woman good day and heads directly toward the other side of town. Toward the Andrews cold storage warehouse.

Chapter 7

Cold Storage

It's mid-afternoon before Jeb finds the icehouse. The building isn't well marked. The wagons out front, piled high with vegetables, made him think at first that the building was some kind of farmers' market. Then he remembers it's cold storage too, not just an icehouse. Some farmers store produce there and sell a little of it each week. He feels silly for having walked by the building twice.

Jeb holds a notebook as he walks around the structure. He also carries a tape measure and a pen. They're mostly props, but he's learned, when doing his labor recruiting, that a man carrying such tools is seldom questioned. He looks official somehow.

But a man carrying nothing, or worse, a man carrying a sack, immediately draws suspicion. He looks like he's up to something.

To further reduce suspicion, he lurks nearby for a half hour. He sits in the open, under a tree, pretending to be a man eating a late lunch and reading a paper. He lurks until he figures out who the official workers are in the building and who's just arriving or leaving in their farm wagons. After he identifies three likely employees, he waits until they're all back inside. He then makes his way along the edge of the warehouse, looking occasionally at the siding and foundation, acting like he's some kind of inspector. He jots fake notes in his book.

The tactic gives him a chance to look through the warehouse windows every few feet. He sees many boxes inside. If he's lucky, the one he seeks will be obvious. If not, he'll have to find an excuse to go inside.

An empty wagon pulls away from the building and turns down the side street where Jeb stands. He nods politely to the driver, and the driver gives a friendly wave in response.

Jeb looks in more windows and sees more boxes. It isn't going to be easy checking this many containers. There are four sets of doors along the side of the long building, and he tries each one, making notes and examining the door casings. Eventually he finds the last door ajar. Earlier he saw men smoking cigars behind the building, and he suspects this is the door they use when they take their breaks.

Jeb quietly slips inside, immediately looking down at his notebook. If anyone catches him, he'll use the excuse that he's looking for the owner and that he must have come through the wrong door. He is a stone mason, he'll say, and he's noticed some cracks in the foundation, which he'd be happy to fix. Right there on his pad are several sketches of the cracked blocks he's noticed.

The workers probably will still throw him out, but throwing out a pushy salesmen is much different from throwing out a thief. He won't suffer a black eye. The worst he'll receive is a little shove, a short lecture about not just walking into the place, and maybe they'll take him up front to meet the owner, who will promptly tell him to get lost.

Emergency exit plan in place, he continues his walk.

Jeb slowly passes through three rooms, identifying two crates as potential targets. They are both water stained and set off by themselves away from the big collection of food crates. In the rear of the third room, he spots another crate and it immediately becomes his top target. Not only water, but salt stains streak across its sides. It's been pushed into a corner all alone, like no one is quite sure what to do with it. He also notices a line of three nails square in the middle

55

of its front panel—a place where the crate would not normally be nailed together. A bit of green cloth hangs from one of the spikes.

Jeb looks left and right. No one around. No sound nearby. He approaches and reads the smeared black stenciling on the bare wood. "Property of Westinghouse Co." He frowns. From the newspapers, he knows that company name. Barely. It has something to do with electricity. Generators maybe.

He isn't sure why such a crate would be on the deck of a ship instead of in the hold. Seems like the owners would want to keep something electrical very safe and away from the water. Or maybe it's just an old crate that someone reused for a different purpose?

Then he remembers that the crates he's looking for belonged to some scientist.

Okay … maybe this is one of them. He approaches the box cautiously.

Voices drift in from a distance. He waits, but they don't get any closer. Jeb scans the room for a piece of metal.

His original plan had been to wait and come back that evening. But he's alone and somewhat protected here in the corner. There is also a loud whine from a steam-driven ice-cutting machine coming from somewhere deep in the building. The droning sound should more than cover any noise he might make trying to open the box.

In the far corner of the room, he spots a small workbench and an unlocked tool locker. Inside the locker he finds a perfect pry bar.

Just as he returns to the corner with the crate, he hears voices behind him. Jeb hastily steps between a row of empty containers and hunches down, peering through the cracks. Three men walk in, laughing, joking, and smelling of beer. They begin sorting through a pile of small containers, swearing and tossing them at each other.

Soon they start piling them in new rows that stretch toward the door.

"When are they picking these up?"

"Ned says before we close!"

"What? All of this? You damn well better be kidding."

"Go complain to him if you don't like it. Order's just been sitting on his table for two days. Now suddenly it's our problem. Says he wants this whole section moved out."

There's more grumbling as they start shoving other crates away from the large group and toward the door. Little by little, the stacks of boxes that provide Jeb with cover begin to disappear.

Chapter 8

Tensions

That evening, Beverly and Jonathan sit quietly in their sumptuous front parlor. Tall windows let warm light fall across exotic carpets. Jonathan rests atop the striped davenport, reading a story from a dog-eared copy of *Lippincott's Monthly*. Beverly, sitting in an upholstered straight-backed chair, is nearby, leafing through a small book of poems. The front cover of the book is white and brown, embossed with flowers.

As the light slowly fades, Jonathan stands, touching a match to one of the gaslights. He adjusts the flame up and back, turning it to just below its smoking point. With polished reflectors mounted directly behind the small flame, the gas lamp immediately sends a rush of radiance into the room.

Finished in the kitchen, Amanda walks to the front door and gazes through the beveled glass. A newsboy is walking past, and she quickly tugs at the brass knob, rushing out to buy a copy of the *Boston Evening Transcript* before the lad can slip away.

Then Amanda joins the Morgans in the parlor, slightly envious of their connubial contentment.

She pulls a few pages out of the newspaper and sits in a chair near Beverly. Something on the remaining pages catches Jonathan's eye. He puts down the *Lippincott's* and scans the newspaper's front page from afar. But Amanda is more interested in Beverly's book.

"What are you reading?" she asks.

"This? Oh, it's a book by a relatively new poet. At least this is new to me. She lived here in Massachusetts, but died a few years ago." Beverly closes the book and looks at its understated front cover. "Someone apparently found hundreds of poems that she had written. Most of them were crammed into a dresser."

Amanda leans forward for a closer look. "That's fascinating. Do you mean she never published any of them?"

"Oh, I think she published a few. But just a handful. Apparently she was content to simply write them and then stash them away."

Amanda tries to return to her newspaper but the thought of the dead poet intrigues her. She finally sets the paper down and asks, "What was her name, this poet, and how did you learn about her?"

"Oh. Well, let's see. I have friend who works over at Roberts Brothers publishers. Someone there read the poems and decided to make a whole book from them. That friend gave me this copy right after the book was printed." Beverly runs her finger over the name on the front cover. "Her name is Emily Dickinson."

"I haven't read much poetry," Amanda admits, "but I guess writing poems is a good thing to be remembered by."

"Yes," Beverly nods and then opens the book again. "Funny thing is, they didn't think there would be a lot of interest. They only printed about 500 copies at first. I heard from my friend that the book is selling so well that they're going to have to print many more. They might even do a second book. They found that many poems, and people do seem to admire what she has to say."

"How about you?" Amanda asks. "Do you like what she says?"

Beverly considers this. "Well, yes actually, I do. She has a remarkable way of cutting right to the quick of things. Emotional and spiritual issues, if you will. The way she thinks and describes those thoughts comes right down on you like a hammer. It's surprising. You're welcome to read it too when I'm finished."

After glancing at the most important stories of the day on the first few pagers of her newspaper, Amanda realizes that she has no further interest in that edition. She wishes instead for a good book, or maybe some embroidery to work on. Something to keep her mind and her hands busy. This seems like the sort of parlor where one can pass the time in many different ways. But as a guest, she's not sure how settled she should become. When she sets her paper on the floor, Jonathan picks up one of the sections.

"Can you read me one of the poems?" she asks Beverly. Over on the sofa, Jonathan grumbles quietly about what he sees in the paper.

"Well, all right, dear," Beverly agrees. "Most of them are rather short, like dainty little gems. But I'm in the middle of one of the longer ones. Let's see, let me pick out a few stanzas." She clears her throat.

"WE outgrow love like other things
And put it in the drawer,
Till it an antique fashion shows
Like costumes grandsires wore"

Beverly flips forward a page. "Let's see … this is part of the same poem, I think."

HE touched me, so I live to know
That such a day, permitted so,
I groped upon his breast.

It was a boundless place to me,

And silenced, as the awful sea

Puts minor streams to rest.

And now, I'm different from before,

As if I breathed superior air,

Or brushed a royal gown;

My feet, too, that had wandered so,

My gypsy face transfigured now

To tenderer renown.

LET me not mar that perfect dream

By an auroral stain,

But so adjust my daily night

That it will come again

Amanda nods, not quite sure she understands the message of the poem. She feels a bit of envy toward those to whom a comprehension of poetry comes quickly. To her, the fractured language and painful intimations of a poem's words are difficult to digest. Yet she empathizes with the nuance of their meaning. They seem to tell about a longing for love that isn't there. Perhaps it never was. Or perhaps love was there once, but now it's gone. But hope remains. Love's absence hangs heavy and colors the hue of the poet's daily continuation.

Amanda's reflection is short-lived.

"Harrison's a fool!" Jonathan bellows with a hiss. He drops the newspaper in his lap.

"What are you on about now, dear?"

"The president! And Cuba! It just doesn't stop down there! He needs to step in, damn it. We all know he does. It's maddening though because he just waits and waits."

"Now, now, dear. It's never a good idea to send our boys to fight. I don't see what the—"

"Baaahhh," he responds with a wave.

Amanda's mind reels as she attempts to shift gears. Pushed from romance to politics. She has read a bit about Cuba, but she realizes her isolated life has kept her from understanding what the issues are. It has kept her from understanding many things. Still, she starts to engage Jonathan in conversation about the problem, much to his delight, apparently. He starts by explaining the history of the island, then works toward the current tensions. Amanda can tell that Beverly doesn't agree with everything her husband says, but she doesn't argue with him.

"Did you know slavery was only abolished in Cuba about five years ago?" Jonathan inquires. "It was one of the few reforms that the Spanish promised and actually carried out! As for the rest? They just ignore everything else that needs to be done. The place needs its independence and for our part, we sure don't need a Spanish colony sitting right off our damn southern shores!"

Amanda listens but soon notices a different sort of tension, right there in the room.

The tension doesn't seem to focus on Beverly's disagreement about sending troops. It's not quite clear what the issue is, but after ten minutes, Amanda decides to excuse herself and wanders up to her room. She stares out the window for a while and eventually considers herself a fool.

The Morgans are not in the custom of renting rooms. They are well off and quite used to their privacy. But her arrival, however graciously they have accepted it, is a bit of an intrusion. Jonathan's delight in talking to Amanda is no doubt a chief cause of Beverly's unease. For some reason, Amanda's chats with Jonathan are different, or interpreted differently, than a friendly chat with Beverly.

Amanda has regarded Jonathan's manner since her arrival as easygoing and paternal. But is she missing something? Is it flirtatious instead, even if innocently flirtatious? (Is there even such a thing?) She isn't good at reading such intent. But if nothing else it reminds her that her transition back to Boston is incomplete, and she needs to find a place of her own. She vows to find a job quickly, even if it's in a dreaded factory. She'll learn to put up with dust, dark windows, and long hours—anything—as long as it means taking that important step toward independence.

Downstairs Beverly and Jonathan continue their conversation.

"Do you know what she asked me today?" Beverly asks, closing her book and placing it on a small table.

"Hum?" Jonathan isn't quite ready to stop his reading.

"She asked me if she could be arrested."

"Oh good heavens," he says, finally looking up. "Why in the world would she be worried about that?"

"I don't know. We've been very charitable to her, Jonathan, but we don't really know the circumstances of her marriage, do we? Or why she left him."

Jonathan peers over the top of his glasses. "She left because he was starting to beat her. You know that, dear. Agnes said that much in her telegram."

"Yes. But why? And why is she worried about the police? Did she assault him too? Did she steal from him?"

"Blast it, I don't know, woman. To me, she seems gentle as a bird. I don't know what she could have stolen because she certainly didn't carry much with her into this house. Frankly I don't see why the police might care."

Beverly nods but gives him a frosty look. "No, she didn't bring much at all, did she?"

She stands, places the poetry book on a table, and starts to leave, plodding with some displeasure across the gaily colored Serapu that decorates the floor. As she reaches the hall, she turns back toward Jonathan, hand resting on the opalescent leaded glass that separates hall from parlor door.

"Do you know what else she asked, dear? She asked me about a man she saw walking down the street. She said she'd seen him a few times and that she had wondered about him."

Jonathan looks up but says nothing.

"I don't know who he was, but he was a very nice-looking gentleman. About her age, I'd say. And that's that. I just thought it was … well, interesting."

"And is it a problem?"

"I don't know. For now, 'interesting' is all I'm saying. I mean, don't you think it is? Here's this woman, broken away from her

64

husband for what—not more than a couple of days? And here she is giving the eye to other men? What does that say about her?" Beverly waves her hand dismissively to emphasize her point. Lace blouse cuffs flap the air like Chinese fans.

Jonathan snorts. "What does it say? It says she's in her early twenties and ready to move on from a bad marriage, Beverly. What do you expect?"

"She is a separated woman. Soon to be divorced. It's nice that we could help, but I'm not happy about having a woman like that in the house. It's bohemian, Jonathan. It's boorish. It's waterfront. Yet you just like to twitter away with her, don't you?" Beverly lets out a long slow sigh. "I realize it's also my Christian duty to help someone in need." She takes another deep breath. "I just don't think it's very discreet to be eyeing strangers on the street, and it's especially not very discreet to be asking about them right out in the open like that."

Jonathan shakes his head, determined not to get more involved in the issue. Disappointed by his lack of engagement, Beverly walks down the hallway toward the kitchen, muttering something to herself about what the neighbors might think.

Chapter 9

Unearthed

"What's it worth to you?" The voice comes from behind Devlin Richards and the words are spoken in a hushed monotone. But the Southerner recognizes the speaker immediately. He turns around to see the face of Patrolman Hudson, walking behind him as the setting sun slowly turns the street into a yellowish haze.

"What do you mean, 'what's what worth?'" He doesn't turn around.

"You know. You and I, we've only met once. We've only talked about one thing. Maybe I have that one thing for you, maybe I don't." Devlin turns enough so that their eyes can meet.

"You tell me what it's worth to you, and I'll let you know what I have."

Devlin stops to lean against a brick wall. It radiates warmth and feels good on his back. The smell of honeysuckle lingers in the air.

"Address of one of the men? And your certainty that it's him? That would mean a lot"

Patrolman Hudson shrugs. "Address? Yes. Certainty that it's him? I could never give you 100%."

"Tell me more. And yes, I'll pay you."

Hudson leans against the wall too. "You got lucky. Since Boston is the capital of the state, information trickles in here from towns around the area. Land records, court cases, things like that. I didn't find any evidence for either of your guys right here in the city. But in the surrounding towns, there were four guys named Peter Jacobs as of the last time a census was taken. There were just two guys named Earl Lindley, and it looks like one of them is dead."

Devlin Richards grows quiet and still. It takes him a moment to ask a follow up question. "So, how old…"

"How old was the Lindley who died? I looked up his obituary. He was 87. Lived just a few doors down from the other Lindley. So the dead Lindley was probably his father. The living one is in his mid-40s. Could be your man."

Devlin scratches his chin. "And you have the address?"

"I do. It ain't Boston. But it's less than two hours ride from here."

"Do you have the addresses for the others? The men named Peter Jacobs?"

"Not so much luck there. Still digging."

The southerner stares toward the setting sun. "What you do have, that would be worth a few coins to me. Yes indeed."

The cop shakes his head. "I think we're talking folding money. Not coins."

"How much do you want?"

"Twenty seems about right."

"Twenty dollars? Are you kidding?" Devlin likely would have paid more, but he doesn't need to admit it.

"Take it or leave it rebel boy. I don't have all day."

"You've already done the leg work. Would be a shame if we called it off and you don't make at least a little money for your effort. How about $10."

"How about fuck you?"

Devlin laughs. "You know your business, I'll give you that. Both sides of it."

Hudson nods. "That I do. That I do."

The money almost imperceptibly changes hands, and Devlin walks away with an address on a piece of paper. But there's no spring in his step. No smile on his face. There's just a grim determination, grown strong over the years due to the weight of its burden.

Chapter 10

Boxes

The slow removal of the crates and barrels in front of him causes Jeb to skitter on his hands and knees toward the rear of his row. He tucks himself behind some older barrels that reek of spoiled meat. He feels himself start to retch but fights the urge to do so. He also fights the urge to move away from the stench because it's his last remaining hiding place.

Jeb isn't quite sure how he ended up here. The plan was to simply allow himself to be caught if someone stumbled upon him in the warehouse. He'd feign indignation and confusion and try to make a sales pitch as part of his cover-up. But instead, he hid, and hiding just makes him look guilty. He made the mistake of thinking he could hide for a just a moment and that the men would move on. Now that his hiding place is disappearing, he regrets his error in judgment.

The trio of workers stays for nearly a half hour, shouting and cursing and pushing things around. Every time the three of them are near the door and away from his area, Jeb puts his shoulder to the rotten meat barrels and tries to move them a bit. He waits until there is some other background noise, and then he shoves as best he can from his sitting position. Eventually he gets three boxes lined up so that they offer a solid screen. He slides himself behind the line and makes himself as small as possible.

Soon there are just two boxes left in front of the barrels. He waits, motionless.

"Wooo-wee!" one of them shouts. "Smell this damn stuff! We can't move this."

"Shit!" says another. "Get those things out of here! How long they been here?"

"No, wait. We've got to load that wagon. Let's leave 'em. We've got practically the whole order filled. We'll clean out those barrels tomorrow."

"They'll stink up the place!"

"Do YOU want to deal with them on this hot day? It should be cooler tomorrow."

Eventually they drag their work outside, and Jeb can hear them loading the items into something—probably a couple big wagons. Slowly they drift away. When Jeb finally creeps out from his hiding place, he reeks from the rot he's been hugging tightly. It sickens him. He kicks the clipboard over toward the crate that he came here to inspect. He bites his lip and tries to keep his cool.

The wagons are out of sight. Jeb decides to lock the door to the other room of the warehouse, but he leaves the back door open in case he needs to escape. A quick look out the window confirms there's no one lurking in the yard next to the building. He can continue looking. At least for now.

Picking up his pry bar, he returns to the water-stained crate that sparked his interest and slams a flat edge of the bar under the top. With a long squeak, it comes loose. He pulls it up and sets it aside. He finds wood shavings inside, matted and tangled from the sea water. He grabs a handful of the shavings and tugs, then laughs to himself as they all pull loose in a single dripping mess. Underneath, there's some kind of strange machinery.

Jeb has never really seen a generator up close. But he's seen sketches of them in books, and he knows this is what one looks like. It's kind of a small version though. Portable.

He pokes around the edges of the box and tears through another wad of packing material. Frustrated, he finds nothing. As he reaches inside, grabbing the generator itself to lift it free, he hears a thumping, dragging noise behind him. Jeb spins around, fumbling for the clipboard as he looks up to see a man step through the door. Jeb clears his throat and mentally prepares his speech. He'll pretend to be with some freight company, sent here to claim a package that was on the *Gossamer*.

But the man is not one of the warehouse workers. This man is leaning on a crutch. His face is pale—at least what Jeb can see of that face through two days' growth of beard. The man's clothes are soaked with sweat. He looks like he hasn't changed them in days. Their eyes meet, and suddenly Jeb realizes who it is.

"You mind telling me," the man wheezes, "who you are, and why you're so goddamn interested in that box?"

Jeb flips through the papers on his clipboard, looking like he's very much on official business. "Actually, I'm in town looking for you, my good man. I'm glad you found me."

"You damn well knowed where I was. Din't ya? That there lady at the doc's office told ya. Din't she! But y'all came on down here instead."

Jeb nods. "Yes. Yes I did."

The sailor squints at him. "Yeah, I thought so. She's a nice lady. She stopped by my place with some soup, and she tells me I had a visitor. But I ain't seen no one come up to my room at all, and I told her that. Then she says you been asking stuff. Asking about this here thing," he gestures toward the crate. "So's I figured I might find you down here instead. First time I been out of bed in days, and look why. You got me up. I had to come out and see what the hell your business is."

Jeb taps this side of the crate. "This must be important to you, this box," Jeb says.

"Never you mind about that. You get away now. Just GET!" He waves his crutch in a threatening manner.

Jeb thinks about challenging him but realizes a noisy fight might draw other people. He decides to play his hand.

"I know about the diamonds."

The surviving sailor, whose name is Toby Bales, looks him in the eye. He squints, a look of anger spreading over his face. "Who the hell are you?"

"A friend."

"Friend? Now there's a load of horseshit."

"Then how else would I know about the diamonds? Hmm? And if I'm not part of the same group of friends, how would I know about you? Of all the floating things you could have grabbed after the wreck, and there must have been dozens of things, you grabbed this box. You nailed yourself to it for Christ's sake. Who ever heard of such a thing?"

"You go to hell. You hear? You just go to hell and you move right away from that crate."

"Okay, okay." Jeb grips the pry bar tightly, just in case he needs it. "But think about this. I don't think those diamonds are in here. You saw I was still looking through it. That means I haven't found them yet. So where are they? Huh? Some other box? Bottom of the sea? Or maybe somewhere else? I know a few things, my good man.

That's why I'm here. I suspect I may know things you don't know. Together, we might find the diamonds, but we have to pool our resources."

The sailor gives him a hardened stare. Jeb raises his hands, shakes his shirt, and turns his pockets inside out. He does everything he can to convince the sailor that he's not holding any booty.

"You see? Nothing! I don't have them. They're not in this wet mess. Maybe they're inside this stupid machine—I don't know. Why don't we pull it out, you and I. We can take it apart and have a look."

The sailor's disappointed, Jeb can tell. In that instance, he also realizes they share the same feeling. Jeb is disappointed too. He was never sure they'd be here, but he certainly hoped they would. It looks like the whole thing may turn out to be a wild and very sorry goose chase.

"Why the hell should I work with you? I don't need you."

"Like I said. You just might."

"Oh. That's right. You 'know things.' So what do you know, huh mister?" The sailor waves a finger at him and teeters a bit, still lacking strength for quick movements. "What is it you're claiming to know, you bastard? Talk fast. I know the people in this building. If I call out, they'll come in here. They'll grab you right fast."

Jeb leans back confidently, arms resting on the open crate. "I know who the guy was who owned this box." He thinks fast, grasping at an idea.

"Oh, you do?"

"Well, yes. I mean, that's why I'm here! I don't know his name, but I know he's an ... umm ... engineer of some sort. Works with electricity. Am I right?"

73

The sailor nods.

"I'm sure you know that, you saw him on the ship. Well, I know some of the men who helped him load this stuff onto the *Gossamer* just before she sailed."

The sailor listens, and Jeb turns on the charm.

"So I sort of feel like I knew him from that. I helped deliver the boxes to the shipyard before they were loaded," he lies.

"So what?"

Jeb continues the lie. "He told me about going to South Africa a few times. He was doing a little trading on the side. On more than one trip too. He sold some diamonds here. He planned to sell some in England too. Someone else told me they thought he was hiding his diamonds in some of the boxes on board. Just like this one. And after all, from the machinery inside, we do know that this was his box."

The sailor squints again.

"Did you see others prowling around the boxes on the ship?" Jeb askes. "Did others know what he had? Did he seem to hover around them protectively when others were nearby?"

"Maybe." The sailor points to the crate. "But you say you ain't found nothing?"

"Nothing. I'm still going to look for more, if you can help. Then I want to go back up to Boston and see if I can track down where he lived. Might be other leads. Might be some stuff there too. And I could always use a partner."

The sailor steps forward to look into the crate. "Never did know for sure. I just sort of hoped there was something in here. That's why I grabbed it when I found it floating. I needed to hang onto something, and I wanted this to be the something." He looks Jeb up and down. "So what the hell do you want to do now? Seems like it's pretty obvious that the diamonds, if there were any, went down with the ship."

"Maybe. But … shit …." Jeb motions for the sailor to step outside with him.

"Look, we're taking a risk by prowling around here. Let's see if we can play it straight and buy the time we need. Let's go up to the front of the building. We'll walk in the front door, find the owner, introduce you, and say you're feeling better in spite of that cough. We'll ask to see this crate. We'll ask officially this time, and they'll say yes because it's basically yours, right? You and the crate were found together, and both brought here to Falmouth. We'll tear the thing apart, every damn piece of it including the generator. We'll look and see what we can find."

"Fuck you. I can do that all myself. I don't need you."

"No? You got the energy to do that, do you?" Jeb looks him up and down. "Look at you. You hardly have the energy to walk. And what about if I tell them I'm here because I think there are some stolen diamonds in the crate? Think that will complicate things for you? Think everyone in the whole place won't want to get involved, or find reasons that they can't give it to you?"

They argue some more, but Jeb's partnership proposal and threats to spill the beans convince the sailor to forge an uneasy alliance.

After quickly tacking the lid back in place, they go together to find the building manager. With his blessing, they spend nearly ninety minutes in the back room, borrowing tools and pretending they want to inspect the seawater-damaged machine to see if it's salvageable. They even take apart the main coil of the generator and sort through all its other parts. They're about to give up when Toby sees something clinging to the base of the generator. He plucks it free. Jeb can see the man's eyes narrow as he inspects it.

"Well, god damn. Look at that."

Jeb looks but doesn't see anything but a sliver of black wood. "Whatcha got there?"

"Piece of ebony. And I sure know where it came from."

"Oh yeah? Is it some sort of big deal?"

"It's just funny, that's all. This guy, this engineer, he had one of those oriental box things. Ever seen them?"

Jeb shrugs.

"You know. They snap apart. He and another guy on board, they both been to Japan sometime in the past year. They had these stupid puzzle boxes. Yeah, that's what they called them. They kept fooling with them, sanding them, borrowing varnish and rubber and shit from the ship's carpenter. Anyway, the guy kept the box near his bunk when he was sleeping and always on deck by the crate when he was working. Finding this piece of wood tells me he might have stored his puzzle box in the crate at some point too, all nice and locked up, but he must have bumped it and a piece came off."

"So?"

"So I think maybe we're focusing on the wrong box. When we thought he kept the diamonds in the crate, he was really keeping them in that little wooden box. Sometimes the box might have been tucked in here. Sometimes it might have been under his bunk. Problem is, that smaller box ain't in here now. I don't think we're going to find it, and I don't think we're going to find the diamonds."

Jeb nods. It makes sense.

"I saw him put something in here," Toby continues, "just before the storm. Then he sealed it up. I thought for sure it was a sack of the diamonds. But later I saw him carrying that stupid box away, down below decks. I didn't think anything of it at the time. But now I think I know what was going on."

Jeb lets out a long sigh. "So if there are no diamonds here, then he probably had them with him, and they're probably lost."

"Yeah. Probably," the sailor sighs. "But maybe not totally lost. I heard the other guy tell a story about those boxes. He said they're a good way to cast your worldly goods onto the water if you know you're going to die. People are more likely to notice and pick up a pretty box, you know? Maybe he had a last will and testament in there too, asking for that box, if found, to be sent to a loved one. Fat chance that anyone who found it would actually do that."

Their eyes met. Jeb's narrow to a slit. "And you think … the diamonds …."

"Tucked inside the box? Floated away? I guess it's possible."

Jeb rubs the bridge of his nose. "Well, if he let it go, we're sunk, literally. We'll never find it, and if someone did find it, they sure as hell aren't going to tell us about it."

They sit on the edge of the crate in silence. Finally Jeb picks up a piece of the generator, eyes it, and tosses it back in the box. "Well, what the hell. I guess it was worth a shot."

As they halfheartedly clean up the mess, he asks Toby what he'll do now.

"I don't know. I won't go back to sea now. Never again." He tries to stand straighter. "I'm getting better. Slowly, I think. Coughing has nearly stopped. Who the hell knows? I don't have a lot of prospects. Over the past several days, I tell you, sometimes I wished the sea had just taken me."

They walk back to the front door and thank the manager. Jeb says the generator isn't salvageable and offers to have the crate hauled away, but the warehouse man says not to bother. They'll just throw it on the cart when they haul away the rotted barrels. It will be dumped in the ocean.

"So where does this partnership go next?" Toby Bales asks after they leave. "What about where he lives? Are we going to try to search it?"

"Oh … yeah. Of course. How long are you going to be staying here in town?"

"Don't rightly know. I figure maybe another month."

"I'll scout things out and send you a telegram. Whether we break in or find a good excuse to have someone let us in, we'll give it a good search."

They walk back toward the center of town. Toby Bales, the sailor, gives a mighty cough, and Jeb feels some guilt about lying to him about keeping him involved. He'll never contact the man again. They shake hands, and Jeb makes a vague promise to send a telegram within the next few days. Not knowing what else to do, Jeb gives the sailor four dollars to help tide him over, then heads back to the train station, hands thrust into his pockets and staring at the road.

Instead of heading home, he hires a wagon and heads as far to the east on the Cape as he can travel. From there, he strikes out on foot, finally reaching the sandy shore. He trudges a couple miles up the beach, with no real hope of finding anything, but knowing he'll feel better having looked for the puzzle box himself. Maybe it washed ashore in a place where no one found it.

Struggling through the deep sand makes Jeb tired. The sand seems deeper here than around Boston. It's like trudging through heavy snow. He's about to turn back when he sees something large and circular in the distance.

Various images fill his head as he moves closer. Is it a discarded round church window? Shopkeeper's sign? Huge millstone? As he approaches, he realizes it's bigger than he thought … maybe a gun turret from a military ship?

Stopping in front of it, his eyes widen as he recognizes the shape. Tipped at an angle against a dune, it looms over his head.

The object is a side paddlewheel, broken loose from a steamer. It's battered, but remarkably intact. Stepping closer, he sees a faded butterfly decorating what's left of its tin cover.

"My God, that has to be from the *Gossamer*," he whispers to himself.

Jeb pokes around the base of the wheel and even climbs on top, but he finds nothing worth salvaging. He searches several hundred yards in every direction, but the eerie, looming wheel is the only piece of wreckage he finds. As the sun sets, Jeb thrusts his hands into his pockets and begins his long walk down the sand, back toward civilization.

Chapter 11

Room for Research

"Yes. Yes, I think this will do nicely."

Nikola Tesla walks the length of a large room, then looks down at a paper in his hand. "If I do agree to the terms, please, how soon can I move in?"

"Since it's empty now," the New York building owner replies, "you can move in as soon as you'd like. Tonight if it suits you, long as you give me a deposit."

Tesla smiles.

"This is a nice space," the landlord continues. "The last tenant made cotton shirts here. Had about a dozen sewing machines set up and a bunch of girls who ran them. There's plenty of room for that." He studies the Serbian engineer with an appraising eye. "But you said you don't plan to manufacture anything here. That right?"

Tesla nods.

"So, mind if I ask you then? What is it you plan to do with this space? What did you mean when you said it would be some sort of lab?"

"Just some research and experiments."

"Not anything that's going to explode, is it?"

Tesla laughs. "Highly unlikely. I work in electricity."

The man's eyes widen. "You don't say? Well ain't that something. I'd love to have electricity in my house. Don't have that yet. But this here factory room is wired! That's how they ran a few of them sewing machines. Started with that about a year ago."

"I know. Having electricity available here already is part of the appeal for me."

"So that's what you do? Research with power and wires and such?"

"And radio."

The landlord looks confused.

"Ever heard of that?"

"Radio? No. Can't say as I have."

Tesla holds his hand to his ear. "Just imagine a telephone. But with no wires."

The landlord raises an eyebrow. "Well that's a strange concept."

"And what if I told you I think I can light up a light bulb without wires too? Using just radio waves. Wouldn't that be something?"

"I don't know. Suppose it would be. Can't quite imagine it."

"And maybe I can carry pictures in the waves too. Or beam power around the world, as far as I want and as much of it as I want, and what's more, I can also …." Tesla's voice suddenly drifts away. He walks toward the window and looks out at the buildings of New York. "So much to do," he whispers. "So many possibilities yet to imagine."

The landlord looks uneasy. "So … you'll take it then? One-year lease, right? No exception. No cancellation, you know."

"Yes. I'll take it. One year is fine."

The landlord smiles. "Excellent. I'll just need you to sign here and give me that deposit."

In less than a half hour, Tesla is on his way to the New York Meatpacking District, to a warehouse where he's temporarily stored his belongings. As the landlord also leaves, he slips the contract back into his pocket, not quite sure what to make of his new tenant, but very happy to have a down payment in his hands. He would have rented it for half the price, just to have it off his hands. It's an awkward space, this long narrow room. But this Mr. Tesla didn't seem to realize that.

Chapter 12

Chronicle

Back in her room, Amanda pulls the puzzle box out of her carpetbag and sits on the edge of her small bed. She studies it for a moment, then begins twisting and turning it until she opens the top compartments and reaches the diary. She stares at the small book for a long time, trying to decide whether to take this journey—to learn more about this unfortunate dead sailor. She decides that she will. After all, why else would he have put the book into a box that someone else might find? She picks it up and, sliding herself up onto the bed, sits back against the pillows with pieces of the box strewn about her lap.

On a whim, she goes to the back then flips slowly toward the front, reading though a couple June entries, then May, then April. She learns a lot. For example, she had assumed that the man was a sailor, but what she reads tells her that he sailed only occasionally, usually traveling for some specific purpose. She also learns that he spent more than two months ashore before heading out to sea for his final, fateful trip. Besides the mention of the June voyage, the only previous mention of sailing was in mid-April.

April 10, 1891

We set sail from Port Elizabeth at six this morning, heading ultimately to Boston, with a stop first in Cuba. The weather has been clear so far, with a low wind out of the southeast. The temperature remains moderate. Thank goodness.

I still can't get over how the seasons are reversed here. It's springtime in my mind because I'm used to Boston. But the air here in the Southern Hemisphere carries a hint of impending winter. Still, we could not have asked for a better day to depart, with the wind just strong enough to carry away the steam and smoke. It trails out behind us, and that always makes the journey more enjoyable.

Within an hour of our departure, we were out of sight of land. I usually find that exciting. It's like the trip isn't really official until the shoreline disappears. It's only then that one starts looking ahead instead of behind.

But this time, instead of looking forward after the land disappeared, I found myself continuing to look back, standing on the aft deck and staring past the stern long after the last dark blotch of land slipped away.

Part of me will miss Africa. Oh yes, the place has its savage moments. I've seen them. The results of the constant tribal battles here are horrendous. Terrible, heartbreaking things. Some of the tribes side with the Boers. Others with the British. Others represent only themselves and a desire for independence.

I've seen bloodstains in the streets. Worse, I've seen dead Zulu rebels, from what remained of their tribe. And, most terrible of all, children without arms—cut off to send a message to an opposing tribe that none of them are safe. It tears one's heart out to see the innocent damaged so horribly. But the violence is not just tribal. The people of the British Cape Colony, the white people, can certainly be just as brutal. Maybe not to the children, yet it's fair to say that whole families were once enslaved on plantations and in mines. And even with formal slavery nearly gone, they still have industrialized the ill-use of people on a grand scale.

Perhaps that's why I did what I did back in Port Elizabeth. Thinking back on it now, I wonder if I did a terrible thing, or if it was something any man in my situation would do. I can't yet decide. I think I need to be far away from Africa before I make up my mind. I know I was driven, in part, by greed. But did that greed make things better or worse for the people I dealt with? What do such dealings do to Africa as a whole? I just don't know. I think that's why I stared behind us for so long as we sailed away. I was trying to figure it all out.

Unfortunately Africa is not a place that makes itself easy to understand. The stories, the nuances, they are all hidden under layers of ceremony and alliances. All I'm left with is trying to understand my own motives. But I'm not sure I'm up to the task.

Amanda swallows hard. A terrible thing? This man? How could he … then she realizes that she really doesn't know this man at all. She's had a vague notion in her head that he was some kind of hero, a good man who went down with a ship. A legend for the ages. But she realizes now this was only a daydream. He was, after all, human. He must have his faults, as all people do.

Outside her window, a group of grayish-purple pigeons has come to roost for the evening. She barely notices them and chooses to read on. She flips back to some of the journal's earlier entries. Perhaps there are other entries that will tell why he thinks he did something terrible.

April 8, 1891

The people I have met here, the ones who aren't caught up in the local tribal battles, seem hardworking, decent, and honest. White, colored, or somewhere in between, most were wonderful people who made me feel quite at home. For them … for their sake, I worry that I may indeed have made the wrong choices.

I guess the question is what I will do with my ill-gotten gains. Will I do good things from here on?

Deep in the recesses of the crates on the deck, I have hidden the diamonds. Dozens of them. They are so easy to obtain in Africa, as long as you have the right things to trade. And I found that I did have the right things. Not guns. No, I wouldn't go that far. Some of the mates on the ship did trade in guns and bullets and powder. But I hated to see that. Blood money, as far as I can see, and I never wanted to deal in death.

I gave them the ability to communicate over distances.

The dark faces who came to visit our ship in the night—the ones who would wait for the harbormaster to finish his patrols and then crawl up close to the port side whispering up to us from the shadows—they needed other things besides weapons. They asked for them by name. They wanted to build their own telegraphs.

I had brought telegraph parts with me. Some for my experiments, some for my work, and some simply because I had heard there's a market for such equipment in Africa. A telegraph wire can stretch deep into the jungle or the grasslands or the desert. It can carry warnings and battle plans. The United States may be moving rapidly toward telephone systems, but the telegraph is only now arriving in the remote parts of Africa. The appetite is insatiable. Communication equipment became my new currency, while their currency was the diamonds to which they had access.

I know little about the men who came to beg and deal for my telegraph parts. All I know is they spoke a little English. I'm neutral enough in their conflict that I would have traded with either side.

Port Elizabeth has a railway connection that reaches north toward Kimberly. That's where the diamond mines are, and many of the diamonds make their way down toward the coast. The men who asked to trade with me were employees of one of the mines that is notorious for mistreating its workers. They pulled stolen gems from their pockets, both cut and uncut, and offered them to me in trade for my telegraph parts. I sold them batteries and generators and brass telegraph keys and receivers. I told myself they deserved to be able to trade their jewels for whatever they wanted. I was just a businessman, correct? I also believed they had the right to steal from the mine owners because of the way they'd been treated there. I was glad to help them. But was my reasoning correct? Or was it just a convenient excuse?

After they were gone, I stood there, looking down at the booty I had obtained. Some rested in my hand, some were spread out on my bunk. I knew I was kidding myself. My desire for riches was as much a part of the trade as any loftier excuse I might piece together. I traded illegally, under the table, away from all eyes, and I made some great deals with shady men.

I make no excuses for my behavior. My desire is simply to enjoy the freedom that riches bring. I broke rules and dealt in danger because I want the freedom to do the research that I want to do. And I never had to trade weapons to do so.

I've had to work hard to make a living. That's not unusual for any man, but it makes me angry — the time I waste on business voyages and installing the same electric generators wherever I go. I have so much else to accomplish with my life. There is no challenge anymore in how I make my living. I should be doing research. On my own terms and in my own place. I should be making progress with Tesla. It's my hope that the diamonds will buy me that freedom, and may God forgive me for my selfishness ....

Amanda looks up from the diary. Who in the world is Tesla? She assumes it's some woman, and her interest grows. "Making progress with Tesla, hmm? Now there's an interesting way to put it. Perhaps this man is a bit of a cad."

She reads on.

I found out just before I left Port Elizabeth that there was a tribal battle just outside the city. Apparently there was some well-coordinated surprise attack. I don't know that I carry any particular blame for the battle because I know none of the details. Yet I have this sick feeling that my new wealth carries with it some kind of blood. Was my equipment used to coordinate the attack? Does it matter to me if it was?

It's a strange feeling, and I don't know where it will lead me.

Amanda looks out at the pigeons and right through them, over the low roof that sits just beyond the window. She's troubled by this traveler's morality. She isn't sure how she feels about the trades he made, especially when he's not sure if the people were hurt. Yet he sold things that could be used for good as well as bad. Is misuse of that equipment really his responsibility? Anything can be a weapon if it's used a certain way, right? Does that mean a businessman shouldn't trade for anything, even things as simple as hammers and nails? This man Victor took a chance, and he made some profitable trades.

And he did feel guilt, didn't he? Does his conscience and his doubt excuse him? She laughs at herself for trying to judge him. She really knows nothing of him at all. Perhaps she can learn more by reading further.

This time she flips forward rather than backward.

June 16, 1891

The sea took a nasty turn today. Rain coming in from the west. It doesn't want to stop, and the swells have been steady for about four hours. At least six people on board have become seasick, including me. I hate it. I hate hugging the rail and feeling green. I hate heaving my breakfast into the sea, and I hate the acid taste it leaves on my tongue. I hate waiting for the feeling to stop, and knowing that it won't. The sickness went on and on for hours.

Now, finally, it's early evening, things have settled a bit, both on the water and in my stomach, and I'm now in my bunk. As I sit here, I also think about how I hate not having any real duties when on board. I'm essentially a paid passenger. The work goes on around me while I wait for my time to —

"Amanda? Are you in there?" The voice at the door is Beverly's. It seems to quiver slightly.

"Yes! I'm in here, Beverly. Do come in."

The older woman enters, smiling a dour smile. She stands for a moment then sits on the edge of the bed.

"I ... I've been talking to one of my neighbors. After you get on your feet, you might want to contact her. She's a widow, and rents rooms."

Amanda nods. "Oh. I ... I will. Yes. Thank you."

Mrs. Morgan looks at her. "I'm not rushing you, dear. Please don't think that. You've been through a lot. You need time. Take it. Find a job that suits you. You are ... of course ... welcome here."

"Yes, but I ... I know I can't stay, Beverly." She touches her hand. "I know that."

Mrs. Morgan swallows and looks at her. "What was it like, with him, dear? Back home. With a man like that?"

"You mean Wayne? My husband?"

The old woman nods.

"Not really as bad as it sounds. I mean, not at first. We had some good times. A couple of good years or more." She looks at Beverly but can't quite get a read on what she might want to know. "But he sort of closed up after a while. Like he didn't want to keep growing with me, does that make sense? The only other thing for him to do, if he couldn't continue, was to pull away. And he did that. Farther and farther, like I was becoming a stranger to him. Then it was like he started to hate me for being that stranger, and I don't know why."

Beverly nods. "I've had times like that too. But Jonathan … he's a good man. He wouldn't let either of us drift too far. And I worked at it too, Lord knows. We started with love. I think that's important. When you start with that, love will stay with you if you treat each other well and do your best with it." She looks at Amanda. "Did you start with love? At least a little?"

It strikes Amanda as an intensely personal question. "I thought I did. I thought he did too. I'm not sure now if that's true."

Mrs. Morgan nods. "Men are weak, you know. I don't mean physically. I mean weak of spirit. They lose their way. They get distracted. Far too easy for them to get distracted, I think, and to stop caring."

"It certainly seems that Jonathan cares for you, Beverly. And you for him."

Beverly holds her gaze as she nods. "Yes. He does. And I do."

And that's where the exploration and the admonition ends. The diary and the open puzzle box catch Beverly's eye. "What's all this?"

Amanda feels slightly embarrassed, then realizes she shouldn't. What she has sprawled, in pieces, across her bed is interesting. Especially the diary. Why not share it?

"It's something I found washed up on the beach several days ago. After a shipwreck."

"Oh dear, was it that steamer that went down off the banks a week or two ago? I read about that. Can't recall the name."

"*Gossamer*?"

"Yes. That's probably the one. So what is it that you found?"

"This." She holds up the main part of the box. "It all snaps together. I've been told it's called a puzzle box." She shows Beverly how it works. "I've opened the first few levels, and that's as far as I've gotten. I found some papers inside, and this diary."

"My! How marvelous. May I?"

Amanda hands her the box. "Oh yes, please." She shows Beverly the diary, telling her that the last entry doesn't really say much; it just mentions that they're heading out from Boston. "This separate note, scrawled on the inner lid, tells what happened after that."

Mrs. Morgan reads the part about *God help us all* and closes her eyes. "That poor man. All those poor souls." She waves her hands in the air. "Why anyone would want to go to sea is beyond me."

Amanda nods, but has nothing to add. She's never understood it herself, even though her family had a history of working on the water.

Beverly stands to leave. "You know, I think Jonathan would be fascinated by this box. Why don't you ...." She pauses for a moment, considering. "Well, yes, why don't you show it to him?"

"Should I? I mean, would that be all right?"

The two woman exchange glances, and Mrs. Morgan nods slowly. Amanda smiles. "Thank you, Beverly. And I will be out of your hair soon. I promise."

Mrs. Morgan hesitates for a moment and gives Amanda a quick, reassuring and sympathetic kiss on the forehead. It makes Amanda feel like a child, but it also eases the sense of apprehension she's felt recently around Beverly.

When Amanda was a child, she had a doll with a smooth porcelain face. Red rouge and painted blue eyes made it the most beautiful thing she had ever seen. The doll became her confidant. In bed at night, beneath the flannel sheets, she told her troubles to the doll. Its blank expression always hinted that the words were heard without judgment. Just having the doll there made her feel better. But she hadn't seen that doll in years.

Amanda picks up the diary and looks at it, feeling, for a fleeting moment, like a diary could serve the same purpose as the doll. She feels that she'll burst if she can't confide in something, anything, just to set her mind at ease

Then she realizes it's not really the diary she wants to talk to. It's Victor himself. But he's long gone.

"It's not my fault." She blinks back her tears as she stares at the small book. In her mind she pictures a man's face, though one that is blurred at its edges. "You know that, don't you? I don't know why it's all happened, but it's not my fault. Not any of it!"

Chapter 13

Quincy

It didn't take two hours to reach the small coastal town south of Boston. The ride took longer. Devlin Richard's borrowed horse didn't help. He was a big handsome beast, but seemed dimwitted and unsure of himself whenever they encountered a little mud. Slowly they plodded onward and eventually clip clopped into the outskirts of town.

Low key. That was the order of the day. For Devlin, there would be no pockets picked here. No cross words for anyone who might get in the way. He decided he wouldn't linger in the shadows nor ride in the sunlight – what there was of it this misty morning. He wanted to look like a man with a purpose, but not so much of a purpose that people would look twice at him.

The trick would be riding up the narrow side road where Lindley lived. As far as he could see, there were only a few houses there, and the old soldier's was likely at the end. Riding up the road and back, just to take a peek, would be far too noticeable in a small town, and especially on this sparsely populated street.

Instead, he ties his horse to a post near the town's general store. He goes inside to browse for a few minutes, buys some bread and smoked beef, then heads back outside.

Instead of returning to his horse, he slips into the woods and walks through the trees, making his way behind the houses along the length of the side rode. Behind the second house an old dog looks up from his nap and barks once, but drops his head back down to his paws, too lazy to investigate.

Devlin makes his way behind the house that he's investigating, the one that may or may not belong to a man that may or may not be Earl Lindley.

It has to be him, Devlin thinks to himself. The name. The location. The fact that there are no others near this age. He may not be able to find that bastard Jacobs, but things are looking good for this damn demon.

He waits in the woods for over 90 minutes. The bread and the salty smoked beef make a fine lunch, but he realizes he should also have bought a drink. They have these strange carbonated fruit flavored drinks here in New England, and he's taken a liking. But since he didn't think of it back at the store, he instead wanders downhill until he finds a tiny creek. Using the palms of his hands he taps into the narrow tickle of water. Just as he brings hands to mouth he hears the opening and closing of a door, coming from the Lindley household.

On hands and knees, creeping ever so quietly back up the small slope, he spots a man near the side of the house. He's saddling a horse and whistling a bit of a tune.

Devlin rummages through the pockets of his coat. Several days ago he found some broken binoculars that someone had thrown in the trash. One side was cracked, but the other seemed useable, so he hacked them apart and kept the good side as a mini telescope.

He trains the device on the man in the yard, and stares for several minutes. It's been many years. Faces have grown fat and hair has grown thin. He wants to be sure. But then he hears him talk to the horse. And when he walks around, he has the opportunity to see the man's face from several angles.

Yes. That's him.

That's the thief.

That's the carpet bagger.

That's the raping son of a bitch who helped deliver a knock-out punch to a family that already was down for the count.

The man climbs onto his mount and yells something to his wife, who leans out a window to answer back. Then he trots out of the yard.

"So where are you going, Earl?" Devlin whispers aloud. "And how about if I come with you?"

Devlin sprints hard back through the woods, to get back to his horse before Lindley passes through town. The old dog barks again, more enthusiastically this time. Devlin winds up and makes a long throw. His last bit of beef lands a few feet in front of the dog and the barking stops immediately.

Chapter 14

Puzzlement

As in many cities, the houses built in Boston between 1865 and 1890 have a much different look from those built in the early part of the century. The newer homes have larger, longer windows – some that look nearly as big as doors. The fronts of these homes often have angled "bay windows" that thrust confidently forward from the rest of the structure. Sometimes these stately bays are covered with copper or tin with decorative ridges or sconces hanging off them like Christmas ornaments.

Such windows remind the world that the residence, and its people, are successful. They are well-off, thank you very much. So successful and assured is this residence that it doesn't have to stay within the confines of its own foundation. The windows reach out. They float. They are a puffed-out chest, assuring the greatness of the place and its family is thrust forward for all to see.

More often than not, when a home has such a hulking bay window, that window is part of its front parlor.

A parlor in a typical 1890s row house is usually the most formal room in the home, filled with camelback sofas, straight-backed chairs, and rows of silver-framed photos atop thick marble mantels. Heavy gold- or silver-trimmed wallpaper may hang like embroidered cobwebs above polished wainscoting. A parlor typically also contains the most expensive lamps a family owns—scattered about on end tables and sideboards—heavy leaded-glass shades that cast swirls of color onto the room's tall ceiling.

The parlor is a place where guests are greeted and where news, good or bad, is shared. Parlors often are dead-end rooms located just off the front hallway, slightly separated from the rest of the home.

These rooms become a world unto themselves, where guests are entertained, where children fear to tread, and where a family's best and bravest face can be shown to the public. Because of this, a parlor may not be a family's favorite room in a household. It's simply a showplace that drips gothic formality. It's not a place where people come to fully relax. Yet, for some families, the room is a bit different. If they have a love of music, maybe if they own a piano, the parlor may become the center of friendship and activity. As a family's social status increases, it becomes increasingly important to have a particularly large parlor to portray the boastful prominence of the home.

The street where Jonathan and Beverly Morgan live contains mostly modest flat-front homes. In the midst of these homes, the Morgans' elegant residence, with not one bay window but two very large ones, shines like a beacon of prosperity.

The home is built of brownstone. The extra-dark red color of its massive blocks is caused by the presence of red iron oxide trapped within the sandstone. The iron acts as a cement of sorts, binding the sand grains together. Sandstone on its own can be weak while brownstone is strong and coveted for building.

Over thousands of years, huge deposits of brownstone collected along the edges of the Connecticut River Valley that runs from New Hampshire down through central Massachusetts and into Connecticut, then on to the sea.

Brownstone has become the fashionable building material of the age, and quarries along the river valley have enjoyed great success, cutting and shipping more and more of the huge blocks. From Boston to New York and beyond, elegant residences have relied on the special brownstones to give their new homes a castle-like facade.

The sweeping bay window on the left side of Jonathan and Beverly Morgan's brownstone accents the lovely front parlor of the residence. The sunny alcove is where Amanda sits on a gold camelback with Jonathan on the warm afternoon of June 30. Before them is a mahogany tilt-top table, set low enough to hold tea. Upon its polished surface rests the puzzle box. Amanda has shown the old man how to open all the compartments down to the diary level. But now her progress is halted. This is as far as she has been able to explore.

Across the table, seated on a couple arrow-back chairs dragged from their usual stations by the far wall, are two other men: a neighbor, Jasper Stokes, whom Jonathan has known for twenty-five years; and Charles, a man who was once a steam-engine mechanic at one of the Boston rail yards. Jasper knows the intelligent but rough-hewn Charles only through his friend and neighbor. But Jasper has asked him to come today, at Jonathan's request. Jonathan picks up the box.

"Very interesting. And this is as far as you've been able to get?"

"Yes sir. No further." She points to the interior. "I don't see anything at all that looks like a release button or a sliding panel or anything. It seems to be a dead end." She watches as he pokes around inside the cube. The visible compartment occupies nearly the top two inches of the eight-inch deep container. There's obviously more space to explore, but he too is unable to gain access. After trying several times, Jonathan decides to call in his reinforcements.

"Have you ever seen one of these before?" he asks the other men.

"No, not really," Jasper admits, examining the box. "I saw something like it at a curiosity shop once. But I never really picked it up to play with it."

After turning it around in his hands several times, Jasper lets out a long sigh. He's stymied. He looks over his reading glasses. "But Charles here used to have a couple of these boxes. They seem to be popular in the trades. That's why we invited him over for this little demonstration. Charles, want to take a crack?"

The old engineer moves his chair closer. He pulls out a brass jeweler's loop and holds the fat side of the lens to his wrinkled eye. He looks all along the interior of the opening. After several minutes, he starts to reminisce about the puzzle boxes he used to own.

"This looks a little like the one I picked up during a visit to Siam back six years ago or so. In fact, I'd say it follows the same basic design."

Amanda leans forward.

"I used to work on a merchant ship back then," Charles explains. "Before I worked at the railroad. A steam engine is a steam engine, you know. Anyway, I remember when I bought it. Oh my. We went on a three-day drunk in Bangkok and stumbled into this little shop. The keeper was just sitting there, smoking opium and looking half-asleep. I'd run through all my money, so I just offered to trade something for it."

"What kind of something?" Jonathan asks.

"Just a cheap railroad pocket watch that I owned. From the Sears Watch Company," Charles laughs. "He seemed to think it was something special, but I'd only paid two dollars for it in Chicago. So it seemed like a dang good trade for me."

Charles runs his finger along the outside of the box, where the inlaid ivory gives way to solid teak. "This box is a little different though. It starts out the same, but looks like someone has modified it. It's a little taller than it should be, and the teak wouldn't be part of the original. My guess is that someone tinkered with it after it was purchased. Because of your story I guess it makes sense that the thing was modified right there on the ship. Makes sense too because there would be pieces of teak available on most ships."

Jasper points to a pair of scars on the teak. "What do you think? Nail holes?"

Charles squints. "Could be. Maybe that part was made out of an old piece of decking." He explores the holes with a thin piece of wire but comes up empty. There doesn't seem to be any sort of button or latch in the opening. He decides to touch the wood along one ridge. "Here, you try it." He hands it to Jasper as Jonathan looks on intently. "My fingers aren't as strong as they used to be."

"Try what?" Jasper peers into the opening.

"Just feel along the edge for a pressure point. As I recall, it's right about here—there should be a slight swelling. No real latch. You just have to sort of bend the edge, and the bottom drops away."

Jasper tries pinching the edge and bends it slightly. There's a soft click. But instead of the bottom dropping away, the front of the box pops forward. Like other panels, this one is protected by a thin rubber seal. Once it's loose, he can literally unscrew the panel, spinning it around a central shaft.

Charles laughs. "Look at that. I guess the design is sort of the same, only different."

Jonathan stands up and walks behind his two friends, leaning against their chairs. "What is it? Can you open all the rest of the compartments from there?"

"I don't know yet. I can see now that someone replaced the area below with this series of … huh. What do you think those are, drawers?"

Jonathan takes the box back and nods. "Sort of looks like that, doesn't it?"

He pokes at the top drawer, then the next. "Nice workmanship. Look how small these are, yet each has a great deal of detail. And the edges are nice and snug." He tugs a little bit on each drawer but none of them budge.

"Teak is good for that," says Charles. "Nice tight joints. Might even be so tight it will be hard to slide those drawers out. That's going to be the challenge here. You won't know if a drawer won't open because you're not doing the puzzle the right way, or just because it's pinched."

Jonathan picks up a letter opener and turns the box on its side. He slowly slides the metal opener into the top of the first drawer, but he can't pry it loose. Exploring around the edge, he strikes something metal and twists. The sound is more like a snap than that of a latch releasing. The front of the drawer flops open at an awkward angle.

"Damn!" Jonathan grunts.

He sets the box down, looking to Amanda with apologetic eyes. "I ... I didn't. I mean ... I wasn't pressing that hard. I'm sorry."

Hand over her mouth, Amanda is silent for several seconds, then realizes she is staring at the damage in horror. She forces a smile. It is, after all, not a big deal. Just a thin piece of broken wood. But part of her feels panicked, like she wants to grab the box and rush it off to some doctor's office. A wood doctor maybe. Someone who can set its broken limb and make it well again.

She takes the box from Jonathan and holds the tiny broken flap like the wing of a bird. "It's ... it's all right," she says unconvincingly. "We had to get it open one way or another ...."

101

Then she notices something inside the drawer. Reaching in, she pinches a short stack of cards. All eyes are on her as she slides them out and sets them on the table. They turn out to be a collection of six brown-and-white stereo-image postcards. The anticipation makes her temporarily forget about the damage.

But the cards are nothing fancy and could be bought at any souvenir shop. This collection seems to represent the places the box owner had visited in his last year or so. There's a brownish double image of Big Ben. There's a double image of Paris looking down a broad avenue of restaurants and shops with the Eiffel Tower in the distance. There's also a card showing what Jonathan thinks is the broad mouth of the San Francisco Bay. He points out that the two shores shown on the card are more than a mile and a half apart.

"You know, people have long talked of building a bridge over that gap, but the water is so deep and fast-moving it would not be an easy undertaking."

Charles nods and says he's only been to the San Francisco side of the bay. "I don't think that could ever be done. I can't imagine a solution for that sort of challenge, least not one that wouldn't bankrupt the whole city."

No one recognizes the other images—probably just local scenes from places in Asia that the box owner had visited. They're cityscapes with signs written in strange symbols—maybe a variant of Chinese.

"Very tough to tell where these are," Jasper laughs. "There are enough stereo cameras in the world now that … well, who knows how many places have been photographed? You can probably find a stereo card for just about anything."

Amanda sees the men look at each other and stifle a few snickers.

Charles picks up the box, examining the drawer front. "I believe this can be fixed." He tugs at the other drawers but isn't able to open them. After Jonathan's experience and Amanda's reaction, he doesn't dare apply force.

"Do you still have your puzzle box, Charles?" Jasper asks.

"No. I cleaned house a while ago and sold a lot of stuff. I brought it to a shop of a man who collects and sells oriental memorabilia. He had several of these boxes when I visited him. All different types. Does a fair trade in them, apparently, though there can't be much money in it."

"Think you could find that shop again?"

"Yes, of course. I know right where it is. It's operated by a curiosity shop owner. Name's Chen Lu. I bring other stuff there now and then. There's a group of shops there, right in a row."

Amanda frowns. "What sorts of things do you bring him?"

"People leave things on the trains. You'd be amazed. Hat boxes. Bird cages. Silver teapots. God knows why they're carrying half the stuff in the first place. We hang onto the items for four weeks. Then we get rid of them. One of the conductors usually volunteers to haul the stuff over to that group of stores. We sell it. We pool the money and use it for a Christmas party every year, or for retirement gifts, gifts for new babies, whatever."

"So where is this place?" Amanda asks.

"It's several blocks west from the Public Garden. Over by the Art Club. Near Exeter and Newbury. It's not really a shopping district. He's on the outskirts of that. He's the sort of place that only the more adventurous wealthy shoppers find. It's where they go if they're looking for an extraordinary bargain, or for something exotic."

Jonathon tucks the tiny broken drawer flap up, then screws the front panel back into place.

"Can you take me there?" Amanda asks anxiously.

"What, today?"

"Yes, yes. Today if you can. Or can you give me detailed directions. I'll go alone. I'd love to have him take a look."

The men just blink at her.

"I keep making a little more progress in opening this box every time someone else takes a look at it. I'm hoping maybe he can help!"

Jonathan looks at the other men. "I don't know. Well, I suppose we could ...."

"Wonderful!" Amanda smiles. "Let me get my handbag and hat."

Chapter 15

Shadowing

Devlin Richards follows Earl Lindley for some time. He always keeps his distance, lingering several hundred feet behind the man wherever he stops. Even though he's stealthy, he's surprised that Lindley seems to lack any sort of personal awareness of threats or safety. If this guy is really an old soldier, he should still have some of that. It never really leaves you.

But maybe this guy wasn't really much of a solider at all. Maybe he was one of those cowards who rushed in near the end of the long war. Devlin knew those types. They signed up after the hard work was done. They came along as the cleanup crew, tapping into the spoils after the battles and reaping a few bragging rights about being there for the final fights – though with little risk to themselves. And the officers. Sometimes they were the worst.

As if to confirm the low opinion Devlin was forming of the man, Lindley stops at a small house near the outskirts of the village. A woman, slightly younger than him, stands at the door, smiling and obviously waiting for him. Lindley looks up and down the street, then pulls his hat low over his brow and heads inside.

Devlin suspects that he has an hour or so before the scum of a man comes back outside. That's fine. He has a short errand to run anyway. He saw an old wagon for sale earlier in the day. Must have been about three streets over. The seller wasn't asking very much.

He could always use a decent wagon. They have so many uses.

Chapter 16

Warrant

The Orleans town constable sighs and removes his wire glasses. Nicotine-stained fingers rub the bridge of his nose.

"Look, Mr. Malcolm, this strikes me more as a problem between you and your wife. I'm not sure I want to get invol—"

"Well, you ARE involved, damn it," Wayne interrupts. "*You* chased her and that other woman down, didn't you? *You* saw how wily and deceptive my wife can be when she wants. She certainly showed you that when she escaped right under your nose. I'm telling you, constable, if she could have killed you, she would have! She's like that."

"Oh, come now, I didn't see anything like that at all."

Wayne Malcolm points his finger at the constable. "Well, I saw it. It was when she stuck me with a knife at home. And I saw it again when she came toward us. You saw nothing? Well, look my scars!"

As Wayne Malcolm sits in the small town hall, he holds his hands high and rolls back his sleeves. The bandages and scabs are an impressive sight.

"Yes, yes. So you've said. But I want you to think about something. Even if I do agree to work with the sheriff and get an arrest warrant issued for her, what good will it do? We have no idea where she went."

"She's not all that far away. Just up in Boston. I'm sure of it. Where else would she go?"

The constable sighs again. "And you think the Boston police are going to just drop everything and track her down for you? I'm sure they've got plenty of their own domestic disputes to contend with."

"Domestic dispute? Can we stop using those words? This is attempted murder, sir! You seem to keep forgetting that part! Or do I need to go to your superior?"

The constable shakes his head and slides open his desk drawer. His anger is apparent as he pulls out a piece of paper. "Very well. Give me all the details again. I'll write it down this time, and I'll see what I can do."

Wayne takes several minutes to tell his story, finishing with their final fight. He then tells how Amanda returned to the house, as he puts it, "To rob me blind before disappearing again."

The constable asks Wayne to sign the document and promises to talk with the local sheriff and possibly send a cable to the Boston police.

"Thank you," Wayne says. He finally seems appeased. "I know you have a tough job. But this one is important."

"And why is it so important to you?" the constable asks, sliding the paper back into a tray on his desk. "What do you hope will happen here?"

"What do you mean? I want justice! I hope to see her punished. Just … just like she's punished me." He sees the skeptical look in the constable's eyes. "I mean it. You don't know what it's like. The constant push-push-push. It was maddening."

"Push?"

Wayne suddenly looks flustered. "For everything. For when I was supposed to plant the crops. For when the hay got into the barn. Other things around the house. All of it."

107

The constable chuckles. "Well, isn't that pretty much what a wife does? I got me a pushy one myself, you know."

"Yeah, well, if you're still hanging on to her, then ain't no way you've been as unlucky as I've been. My woman must be cursed or something. Pushed real hard. About everything. She drained me. Everywhere."

The constable laughs out loud. "Everywhere?"

Wayne turns beet red and stands up, grabbing his hat. "Like I said. You don't know what it's like. I pray that you don't ever know, sir. It ain't a pretty thing."

"Well, I guess I can understand that," the constable smirks. "If you don't want that sort of thing."

The door slams, barely covering the constable's chuckle as Wayne hurries away.

Chapter 17

The Ride

Devlin has a minimal harness that he's rigged up from pieces of old rope. It's enough to get his horse to pull the wagon, at least as far as he'll need to go tonight.

As he hoped, he returns to find Lindley's horse still tied outside of his paramour's home. He parks around the corner and waits. It will be dark soon. So much the better. Let the Yankee have his fun. Maybe he'll be all the more lazy and preoccupied when they meet.

As the light grows dim Devlin slips into the yard, offers half of an old apple to Lindley's horse, then unties him, leading him off to another yard. Then he turns his wagon around and moves it up the street. If and when Lindley emerges, he'll start down the street, looking to all the world like he just happens to be riding by.

It takes a while, but the man does indeed emerge. Devlin can't hear much from this distance, but he's pretty sure there's some surprise and swearing. He lets it go on for a bit, until he can make out the shadow of Lindley walking toward the road, calling his horse's name.

"Skyler!" He whistles loudly and calls several more times. Devlin snaps the reigns and starts his journey. It's a short trip, but one he's waited for, for such a long time.

He and his horse slowly trot up the road. He reaches Lindley, who's still calling Sklyer's name.

"Lose something?" Devlin calls out in the dark.

"My ride!" Lindley answers. My horse. Had him tied right here. If someone stole him, so help me I…"

"Light brown gelding? About 14 hands high?"

"What? Why, yes? Black stocking on the two front legs?"

"Yes indeed!" Devlin responds, "Saw him about a quarter mile up the road. Just grazing on the side. Must have gotten loose."

"Huh. I don't understand that. He was tied pretty good."

"Well, you know how those fool beasts can be. They get a whiff of something they think they'll like and they can pull pretty damn hard to get free. Do you want a ride back up there? Don't matter none to me. I can turn around. Glad to help."

"Sure," Lindley replies. "That would be right nice. Appreciate it."

He climbs up onto the front buckboard next to Devlin. A partial moon is coming up over the salt marches on the edge of town and the glow paints everything with a powdered sugar sort of glow.

"Don't think I know you stranger. You from around here?"

"Well, not really," Devlin replies. "I've been fixing to move here for some time and I just got here about two days ago. I'm joining my cousin and his family as a hired hand."

"Oh? They run a farm?"

"Well, not much of one. Not yet anyway."

"What's your cousin's name? I probably know him."

They turn a corner onto a narrower road, where the bushes grow tight to the shoulder and the light grows dim through the leaves.

"You know, you probably do know him. But instead of telling you his name, let's see if you recognize him. When I was in town today they asked me to pick up a brand new family photograph that they had taken last week. The photographer took a few days to develop it. Here, it's right in my pocket.

"Ha. Well, okay… Not sure if I'll be able to see it in this light."

Devlin reaches into his coat pocket.

"Wait. Didn't Yardmoore's photography shop close a few months ago?"

The hand exits Devlin's coat quickly, holding not a photograph but a stout iron bar that's only 10 inches long. It's hefty, and with a swift and sure placement, the bar strikes Lindley on the side of his head with a thud, sending him sprawling backwards into the bed of the wagon.

Devlin doesn't bother to slow the horse's trot. He loops the reigns onto the seat and launches himself back into the wagon bed, landing on top of Lindley. He's ready for a fight, but it turns out to be minimal. The man is groggy and confused from the blow. He attempts to throw a couple of ineffective punches then passes out.

Devlin ties Lindley's hands and feet and stuffs a rag in his mouth, holding that in place with another rope.

Done. That Yankee won't go anywhere. The trick will be to get to where he's going before Lindley wakes up. He deftly turns the horse and wagon and makes his way toward Quincy Point and the Weymouth Fore River.

Chapter 18

Ballast

Following the edge of the Weymouth Fore River, Devlin comes to a heavily industrialized area with run-down docks and piles of coal. The area is quiet, save for a small fishing boat that sits idling at the end of a long pier. He drives well past this spot, then slows... eyes scanning the water's edge, looking closely at piles of debris until he spots what he's looking for.

Lindley stirs in the bed of the wagon. But he doesn't seem fully conscious.

Devlin walks to the pile and pulls out one, then two, bulky and heavy items. With a satisfied smile, he carries them one by one to the end of a different empty pier. After setting them on the edge, he lights a cigarette and watches until the fishing boat pulls away.

While standing there, he notices a small movement out of the corner of his left eye. He turns quickly, but it's only a cormorant standing on the shore. The gangly black bird hops and flops in place. The movement makes no sense until Devlin sees that its wing and a webbed foot are tangled in a net – one that probably came from an old lobster trap.

Devlin walks in that direction. "Huh. Trapped, are you? How are you going to get out of that one?" He watches the bird struggle for a moment. With a chuckle he pulls out his knife. Grabbing the bird, he pins it to the ground, stares at it for a moment, and then cuts away the netting. When the bird is released it stumbles forward, shakes its head and flaps its wings a few times. Then it looks back at Devlin before turning toward the river. With a few hearty flaps it heads out, fast and low over the water until it disappears from view.

Devlin returns to the pile and rummages around, eventually finding two more flat items. These too are carried to the end of the pier.

Back at the cart, he finds Lindley awake now, and looking very confused. Devlin holds the man's face, gives him a little smile and a nod. Pats his cheek, then climbs into the seat. With a little effort he gets the clumsy horse to back the cart onto the pier. But the beast whines and hesitates once he's over the water. Devlin unhooks the cart and ties off the horse. He can push the cart out to the end of the pier by himself.

"Bet you're wondering what's going on, aren't you?" He calls to Lindley. The only response is a panicked whimper. "Oh my. So much to explain to you. I'd take that gag out of your mouth, but I really don't want to listen to your damn voice."

At the end of the pier the wheels bump up against the bulky items he placed there. They're flat wide cobbles weighing about 50 pounds apiece.

"Now, my good Mr. Lindley, when we were first heading down here, I thought I was going to have to use the makeshift reigns that I created for my horse here. That would have been fine. I could have come up with some plan on how to use this wagon. But, the nice thing about being near the water front is that there's always ropes and crap just lying around. Why, right here at the base of this dock I found some lobster traps and several connecting lines. Isn't that great?"

Lindley's eyes grow wide.

He pats the man's head. "You don't know who I am, do you?'

The man urgently shakes his head.

"Well, I recognize you. Yes I do. You're older now. But in the moonlight I definitely can see that it's you. I want you to think back… back to the war. Back to when you were in South Carolina. Charleston actually. Remember that Marching into Charleston like you actually had something to do with that capture? Traveling with that nigger regiment? Hum? That's easy to remember, isn't it?"

Lindley blinks several times. Devlin makes a loop with the rope.

"Now, it's not enough that you destroyed my family business, you and your Union fucks. You came to my house too, my good man. You stole my things. Silver. Money. Paintings. And if that wasn't enough, you had your way with my sister. Do you remember now, Mr. Lindley? Do you?"

The man screams into the gag, twisting and contorting urgently. But Devlin calmly continues to measure his rope and tie his knots.

"Now these stones right here. Do you know anything about them? These stones are used for ballast. You know, down in the holds of ships. Well, maybe they're not used so much anymore because ships have gone all steel and the designers now pay a lot more attention to how they're balanced. But these stones still have their uses. Any good shipyard – doesn't matter if it's here in New England or down south – tends to be littered with these damn things. Piles of them. They're nice and square, so some of them end up being reused for roads or foundations. Did you ever see that Mr. Lindley? You've probably walked on them. But some of them still lay around the ship yards. Just sitting there, all nice and heavy, for years. Until someone finds another use for them."

Devlin looks at Lindley and smiles. The man screams again, then eventually goes quiet, watching Devlin work.

"Now, what caught my eye about these stones, as opposed to the others in that pile, is that they're notched on either side. See that? That was so the stones could be tied in place. That's a good careful

114

captain right there. Can't have your ballast sliding around and causing your ship to list." He ties a rope around all four of the stones, cinching them together in a solid clump.

Devlin Richards then climbs up into the bed of the wagon, where he jerks the rope and rag from Lindley's mouth. "Nothing to say?"

"Help!!!" Lindley screams. "Somebody help! Please help!" the words echo against distant buildings.

Devlin stands high in the wagon, arms outstretched. He spins around. "Can anyone hear this man's pleas? He needs help. Anyone? Anyone at all?"

There is no answer, except for the waves lapping at the shore.

"I guess there's no one. Sorry." He runs a rope between the stones and Lindley's feet, with about five feet of slack between them.

"Please," Lindley says. "Please don't do this. Please!"

Devlin nods. "Hum 'please.' I remember that word. I had to listen to my sister shout it several times. You remember my sister. Pretty thing. You two were quite intimate for a short period of time, though not by her choice."

Lindley looks away.

"I couldn't help her though. So I thought maybe, just maybe, the word please would mean something to your friend who held the gun on me. So I said it directly to him. It didn't mean anything to him either. He just watched me. You carried on."

"It wasn't me."

"It sure as fuck was."

115

Fear and panic are evident in Lindley's eyes. But he tries to sound rational. "I'm sorry. Okay? What can I say? It was war. We all saw shit. We all did shit. We changed. I'm just… I'm sorry."

"Ah yes. We changed. You now who really changed? My sister. After that day, she was just a shell of herself. For a long time. Didn't want to talk. Didn't want to look at anyone. Just sad really. And then slowly, after about 18 months, she changed again. Threw herself into her work. The old family business was gone. So she found a new way to make money. Kept books for the few businesses that had survived. She changed inside too. She didn't blame those men. No. You know what was strange? She started to blame us. The family. What we stood for. We caused it, she said. She pulled away from all of it. Even married a Yankee eventually. Can you believe that? What a sick twist that was."

"Look. I have money. Lots of money. I can show you where I have it. It's yours if you want it. Let's go get it now."

"Money?" Is that what you think this is about? Fuck your money. Oh, and it wasn't just my sister whose life changed. I had no more family business to inherit. No prospects. Nothing. I had 25 years of odd jobs and ditch digging and eventually picking pockets and living out of jail cells for a few months at a time. No life. No wife."

Devlin double checks the ropes. Lindley continues to beg for his life. Right up until the point where Devlin starts to drag him toward the tail of the wagon. He gives the man a final wicked smile as Lindley howls and shrieks.

Then, a strange quiet sets in. The two men look at each other as Devlin pulls hard his final knot.

"We knew who you were, you know."

"Hum?"

"We knew. At least, we knew the family. We knew the business you were in. That's why we chose your house."

Devlin gives him a blank look.

"When you oversee a Regiment like the 55th, you hear the men's stories. Several of them were escaped slaves you know. We heard about all of it. They wanted revenge. They wanted an up-close look at someone who was in your business. Slaving. They would have ripped you apart if we let them. But we had barely taken the city. Letting that group kill and loot right in the center of town, well, that would have stirred up some might big issues. We needed a different method.'

"So you took the spoils for yourself, you bastard."

"We told them we would. They were listening. But, hell, you lived through it. You're alive. Your sister is alive. They would have slit your throat. You're welcome."

Devlin seethes. He stands in the bed of the cart and kicks Lindley squarely in the groin.

"Fucker…. Ummppphhh" Lindley turns on his side and breaths deeply. "I didn't ruin you. I didn't ruin your family. You were ruined long before we got there. God has no mercy on the souls of men who put other men in chains. He has no place for those who buy and sell those men like bales of cotton."

"Shut your damn mouth." Devlin kicks again. "Don't you dare tell me about what God wants or doesn't want."

"You've been waiting for revenge all this time?" Lindley says, tears welling up in his eyes. "That's the saddest damn thing I've ever heard. You're going to kill me? Why don't you kill yourself? Can you? Or maybe you're already dead, and you're just looking to take someone else with you.

Devlin jumps off the cart. He places his foot against the wad of stones. "I promised a man that no body would be found. How deep do you think it is off the end of this nice long pier? Maybe 18 feet? It's high tide right now. I think it might be over that." He gives the stones a mighty shove and they tumble off the end of the dock. "Go to hell Lindley."

As the stones drop fast, Lindley is pulled, feet first, out of the wagon. He bounces off the edge of the pier and slides quickly into the water. Devlin steps forward to watch him sink. Panicked eyes look up at him through the salty brine. Lindley is pulled down quickly and a long stream of bubbles flows from his mouth. It's an underwater scream that can't be heard.

Chapter 19

Arrangement

"To say that I'm disappointed would be a considerable understatement."

Devlin Richards gazes across the large Rose Point table to stare Jeb Thomas down. It's not often that Jeb looks away from a challenging gaze, but Devlin's piercing brown eyes make him uneasy. He looks toward the bartender instead.

"Well, we knew it was a long shot. I paid you for your time. But the bigger payoff never materialized."

Devlin touches the tips of his fingers together. He stares for so long that Jeb begins to wonder if the man has slipped into some kind of trance. When he finally speaks, his words come out wrapped in accusation and spite.

"Or so you say. Hmm? You say you found nothing. But then, are you the type of man who would admit it if he'd just found a fortune? Are you the kind of man who would keep his agreement and share it? I think not. I think you'd simply pretend that you found nothing. And that's right where we are now, isn't it?" *God damn Massachusetts. Why do things always have to be so difficult here?*

Jeb looks back, putting on his best negotiator's face. "Have you considered that if I had managed to find a fortune, I might not have come back at all? Maybe I'd have been on the next train back to Chicago and you would never have seen me again!"

Devlin considers this.

Jeb sees that this line of thought may be his best opportunity. He presses on. "I should think the fact that I came back at all, to talk with you and to settle our accounts, is an indication that I'm showing good faith in this arrangement. No?"

Devlin takes a sip of whiskey and wipes his mouth on his sleeve. "You found something there. You stayed for over three days. Why was that, and what the hell did you find?"

"Nothing. I already told you."

Devlin slides a knife out of his boot and starts cleaning his fingernails. Jeb leans back in his chair. He tries to display an aloof, fed-up look. But … that knife. He recognizes it as the long throwing type. Nicely balanced, and with a full metal shank, it can be flung quite accurately by someone who's had a bit of practicing.

"This is the same knife I showed to our mutual friend, Mr. Baines," Devlin smiles. "Do you remember that night?"

Jeb nods. "Indeed I do."

"You followed me that night, right? Makes good sense to follow a man you don't trust, don't you think? Or to have him followed?"

No response.

"A sailor friend of mine knows the blacksmith in Woods Hole," Devlin continues, "not far away from where you went. I tracked down his address and sent him a telegraph. Had him check up on you while you were in Falmouth. He told me about your visit to the warehouse and how you and that sailor took some strange machine apart."

Jeb gives him an icy look.

"Must be some reason you left that part out of your report, hmm, Mr. Thomas? You told me you didn't find anyone or anything."

Jeb suddenly feels very thirsty. He motions to the bartender to bring another beer. He's not sure if he really wants the drink, or if he just wants another person nearby as a precaution.

"I didn't tell you about it because nothing happened. It was a complete wild-goose chase."

"That why you went for a walk on the beach after that? All part of the same goose chase?"

Jeb slaps the table. "Yes, as a matter of fact, it was. Look, we're partners. I'll level with you. I looked for a treasure in the box and found nothing. Then I looked inside the machine that we found inside the box. Still nothing. But I did find a sliver of wood, and the half-drowned sailor told some story about a different box that the engineer had with him. Smaller. Just a toy box of some sort. He suspected *that* was where the guy kept the diamonds. But that box was gone. It was the only lead we found, so I decided to take a walk on the beach. Just wanted to see if, by some miracle, that other box had washed ashore."

Devlin nods.

"I traveled up to the eastern edge of the Cape," Jeb continues, "and walked for a couple miles along the beach. Up to where most of the wreck came ashore. But there was a pretty thin chance of finding anything. No luck at all. Beach was picked clean, save for the massive paddlewheel. Now I'm back here and nowhere else. I'm telling you the whole damn story because I thought we were partners and I thought you should know, and that's the end of it."

"Another box, hmm?"

"That's what I said."

"A toy box?"

"Something like that."

121

"Ahh." Devlin continues to tap his fingers. The silence lingers. "Fine." He finally asks, "Tell me more about this toy."

After Jeb explains it, Devlin seems to understand, and the ideas rush in like a vacuum has suddenly cracked open.

"So if someone found this box, do you think they'd just bust it apart to get what's inside? Or would they be able to open it using the steps of the supposed puzzle."

"I don't have any idea. I have zero information about how it works."

"Well, from what I know of those puzzle things, they can be pretty difficult. The builders make them hard on purpose. Assuming someone found it, and assuming whoever found it doesn't just knock it apart, they may not yet know what's inside. And if the puzzle is difficult enough, they might need help."

Jeb nods slowly. He doesn't understand what Devlin is driving at, but he knows that the man's anger and focus have turned elsewhere. He feels safer.

"So tell me. Do you think that this box survived? Or did it go down with the ship?"

"I don't know. I don't think anyone does."

"Have a gut feeling?"

"Just a feeling? I'd say it's fifty-fifty. We know he tended to carry the little box with him, and that is wasn't placed in the big crate before the wreck. So it had to either be left on the deck or taken down below. If it was on deck, then yes, it floated away. Down below? Very little chance that the box ever made it out. You know that."

Devlin nods, eyes half-closed. "Box like that has diamonds in it, would you let it out of your sight? Just leave it unattended?"

"Probably not."

"So the question is, was this scientist gentleman on the deck, or was he below when the ship went down?"

"His body hasn't been found. I don't think anyone would have stayed on the deck in a storm like that. In fact, I'm sure that's why he took the box out of the big crate. Even if the big crate was lashed down, he didn't want his little treasure to be on deck at all."

They catch each other's eyes.

"That's the story then, isn't it?" Jeb sighs. "It probably was below decks, and it probably went down with the ship. 'Cept for one thing. We knew there was talk that it was the sort of thing some sailors would set loose if the end was coming. So maybe he did that. And that delicious *maybe* was enough to make me go wander up the beach to see what I could find. But *maybe* can only carry you so far. And maybe someone else found it first."

Devlin nods, then spits tobacco juice in the general direction of a tarnished spittoon.

"Tell you what. There's a well-known curio dealer in town who collects those puzzle things. He's the only real expert around. So if it was found, anyone who's trying to go by the numbers and open it the right way is eventually going to track down an expert for help. Or, if they don't care about the thing, they might decide to sell it whole, rather than smashing it up."

Jeb laughs. "So at the very least …."

"At the very least, I want this shopkeeper to be on the lookout. If anyone comes in with a box they found, or one that even looks like it's got some saltwater stains, I want him to contact me."

"Contact us," Jeb whispers. "I told you all of this because we're still partners, right?"

Devlin says nothing, but slowly finishes picking at his fingers and puts the knife away.

"All right then," Jeb says in a relieved voice. "When will you go to see this man?"

"In a few days. His shop is closed until then."

Jeb realizes this means he has to stay in town for a few more days. His funds are tight, but he's staying in a cheap place that rents rooms to sailors, and he should be able to stretch his limited funds.

"Everything all right then? Between us?"

Devlin nods. "For now it is. Don't you cross me again though."

"Again? I never have crossed you, sir. I never will. I believe you're counting on that commitment, no?"

"Indeed I am."

Jeb leans forward. Daring to establish his own sense of authority over the situation, he looks the southerner in the eyes. "As am I, Mr. Richards. As am I."

Chapter 20

Journeys

Amanda's trip to the curio shop turned out to be a waste of time. The owner had closed it up tight for a few days. Instead, she returns to her house and opens the diary.

From the diary of Victor Marius

April 27, 1891 – Off the east coast of Florida

We are just two days away from our arrival in Cuba. It's late afternoon, and I simply roam the ship, talking, reading, and doing what I can to help. I have no formal duties here. I wish Westinghouse would spend the money necessary to let me travel on regular passenger ships. I'd at least have other paying passengers to talk to. But because I travel with such volumes of electrical equipment, the company usually makes a deal with one freight company or another, and hauling our boxes usually includes free passage for me. Being the only non-sailor along for the ride makes for a pretty boring trip, but I find my own ways to occupy my time.

I think it's around four o'clock right now, though I'm not entirely sure, having left my pocket watch down below in my locker. It's far too hot below the decks. The airflow there seems nonexistent. The smell is retched. Instead, I'm sitting topside on a coil of rope that's thankfully tucked into a shady corner near the wheelhouse.

Topside definitely is the place to be when a ship enters the warmer waters. I have never seen an ocean this blue, like a brilliant royal cloth rolled out endlessly toward the horizon. We've passed a few tiny islands. The sand is bright white around here, and the water is astoundingly clear, with virtually no suspended particles of dirt or algae. The effect is strange. Sunlight passes through the water and reaches down thirty, maybe even fifty feet. It illuminates the bottom just like you're peering into a jug of fresh spring water. The ocean simply glows, and the blue reminds me of the sparks that jump from the contacts of my generator. It's that bright, and maybe even that electric.

Also, while it's oppressively hot, the beauty of the place encourages one to tolerate the heat. If it weren't for that, this stretch of open water might indeed be unbearable.

Most of the crew works without their shirts. They too lurk in the shadows when they can, and they're constantly dipping buckets overboard and drawing them up with ropes, dumping the water over their heads and splashing each other. Anything to stay cool. Other than minimal work, we all keep our movements to a minimum. There is a small but steady north wind, thank God, so we seem to be moving at a healthy clip. Besides the paddlewheels, we've also hoisted a small sail on the spar of the mizzen mast. Every little bit helps boost us along.

I'm very much looking forward to Cuba. Maybe I'm just excited by the exotic promise of the place. I haven't been in a truly foreign land since visiting Japan.

Australia, England, South Africa—I suppose those were foreign to me too, yet all seemed strangely familiar. I knew the main language. I understood the prevailing customs. I could read the signs and navigate their cities with little difficulty.

But a country like Cuba—with its completely different language, customs, and mores—that is a treat, and it can be a scary one.

I've been practicing my Spanish with Enrique, the ship's assistant cook. When we land, I think I'll know enough basic phrases to travel around a bit on my own. At least I'll be able to ask for food and drink and hopefully directions back to the ship.

So I'll do just that. I need to get away from the ship and the docks. I need to lose myself for a while in Cuba. I need to let an exotic world wash over me. Maybe even hide me. I think I need to be removed for a time—from the customs and expectations of my own culture—because they've somehow grown to confuse and worry me.

I think I'm still haunted by the decisions I made. I still remember the gunshots I heard late at night. I remember the pain I saw in people's eyes. I realized that I was a trespasser. Part of a long line of trespassers. The riches I found in my travels, the diamonds in my possession, the decisions I made, are all jumbled together in my mind. I know—I absolutely know—that my trade helped escalate, in some small way, a conflict that continues to tear nations and people apart. Thankfully, I sold no weapons. No direct guilt there. But I did provide the powerful arsenal of information and long-distance communication. Had these tools simply been used defensively, I'd be proud of my participation. But I suspect they were used differently, to carry messages about attacks and deadly strategy. I must accept that I may have added to that country's pain and suffering. And I took loot to boot.

But that's enough obsessing for now. I do need to escape. Cuba indeed will be good for me, and they say the big island should appear over the horizon within the hour.

Amanda closes the diary.

The gas pipes in the Morgans' home do not reach to the top floor, so she reads each night by lamplight. She lets the musty book drop to her chest. The old-style whale-oil lantern on her nightstand casts a trembling shadow off the peak of the book. This silhouette

127

stretches down her flat stomach and between her legs, ending near her ankles. She sighs. Farther down, beyond the iron footboard, a sheer curtain blows softly. The night is warm. A dozen crickets stridulate somewhere below—lone males hiding in moist corners of the alley—calling out for company and hoping they'll be heard.

It's after midnight, but sleep holds no enticement. Amanda lies quietly in her bed, half reading, half making plans for tomorrow. She has to find a job. Then a place to live. At some point she must find a lawyer, though she can scarcely afford one, to plan a proper end to her life as Mrs. Wayne Malcolm.

This wasn't a place she ever expected to be. Maybe she should become Amanda Grant again? Or perhaps choose some other name? What is the proper protocol for such things? Most women who break from their husbands simply drift away, but remain married in name. When people ask what happened, they simply say things like "His business took him away" or "He had family obligations in another city." But Amanda doesn't want that sort of open-ended continuum. She's young. She still has time to build a new life. With some surprise she realizes that she's never known another divorced women. It simply isn't done. Permanent separation is the only alternative. She feels like a singularity. An enigma with no one to turn to for advice.

Sometimes she envies the dead.

Amanda strokes the spine of the journal to remind herself of the peace that at least one dead man must now feel. There definitely are no worries about the future for Mr. Victor Marius. His writings betray that he may have felt guilt once, but that feeling has slipped away. He feels no feelings now. No guilt. No shame. No scandal.

After staring at the ceiling for a while, she knows what she must do. Obviously she must find a job. But it must be a job that also includes room and board—that would solve two problems for her. Such an arrangement would allow her to move out sooner rather than later.

So what kind of job might that be? A few obvious things come to mind. Chambermaid in some big hotel? That might work. Some of the nicer ones provide rooms for their workers. She speaks English, which could put her in line in front of some of the recent immigrants who often are favored for such jobs. She also could be a housemaid at one of the Beacon Hill mansions. But those jobs are much harder to come by. She'd need contacts and references just to get an interview. Yet is the life of a maid even one to which she could aspire? That's the very type of life she was hoping to avoid when she originally left Boston and then again when she left Cape Cod. It would be sad if that's where she ended up anyway.

Amanda picks up the diary and starts to read again. Victor writes of arriving in Cuba, and of the lush banks of tropical flowers that seem to roll down the hillsides. He describes the palms— hundreds of them—arching over the water, beckoning the ship toward port.

As much as she envied his deathly peace a moment ago, she now envies the freedom and wonder he must have felt when visiting the tropical port. She has never traveled like that, nor seen such places. She's never even been outside Massachusetts.

Amanda again remembers standing on the shore of the Cape, thinking of how large America has become, and of all the places she's never been. Maybe escaping from New England should be part of her plan? Should she see more of what's out there?

A sailor's life, hard as it is, would be a great escape too. How unfortunate it is that women sailors are nearly nonexistent. She smiles slightly, wondering how safe females really are aboard a ship. All those men. All that time at sea. A woman might have to board herself into her bunk just to stay safe.

Ah, but the chance to travel. That is attractive. She's already enjoyed the small amount of traveling she experienced just driving the steam wagon up to Boston and having that small level of control over her destiny. It gave her a thrill like she'd never known. The passing scenery. The stunned looks from strangers.

She pauses for a moment to think about which jobs she could find that might include traveling. Could that also, somehow, include room and board?

Working on a passenger ship maybe? But what if she ends up like the poor passengers of the *Gossamer*? No, to live on the sea doesn't seem attractive to her.

One other job with the promise of travel occurs to her, but she laughs it off. What about the bordellos out West? Those places are always looking for women. Women of all ages. She's seen very discreet ads in newspapers that fool no one. Western hotels looking for hostesses. Some offer free rooms as part of the deal. Some even offer a girl cross-country train fare and "a new set of clothes."

She smiles and thanks her good Christian upbringing for keeping her away from such paths. Still, a small part of her wonders what sort of life that might be. Would it be so bad? No one would know her way out West. Who would care what sort of reputation she might have? But she would have to deal with the sweaty, unshaven cowboys. The lonely old men. The thieves looking to trick a woman into giving a free favor before disappearing. Yet wouldn't there also be an occasional gem? Maybe a good, hardworking man, lost in the West and looking for a woman just like her?

Amanda shakes her head. She's a daydreaming fool! Such men don't stumble through bordello doors, and if they do, they're certainly not there to look for a wife. It's not a place where an honest woman would ever search for a good man.

Then Amanda blinks.

The whole idea of "free train fare" suddenly stokes a completely different idea. It's a silly idea really, and she laughs at it. At least at first. But the more she thinks about it, the more logical it seems.

She knows she'd rather be a shop girl than a maid, but she very well may have to take a maid's role. If so, then why not become a traveling maid? Why not a maid on a train? The newer trains have sleeping cars. Many of them have maids who live and work right on board. Is the idea so far-fetched? It would get her out of the Morgans' house. It would give her a place to live. It also would give her a paycheck and provide a coveted chance to travel—all rolled into one. It was a perfect opportunity to see the world, and a perfect escape for her. Why hadn't she thought of this before?

She sits up in bed, too excited now to sleep. So much to consider.

After traveling by train for a while, who knows? Maybe she could find a job in some hotel in a distant city. Maybe a resort town. The possibilities suddenly seem as broad as the country, and as numerous as the towns that dot the American landscape.

Smiling in satisfaction, Amanda reads some more of the diary, learning about the Cuban people. Within the pages, Victor confesses to being smitten with a certain young woman who works in a shop near the docks. As the ship ends up delayed in port for nearly two weeks, he mentions several visits to see her. Amanda wonders how far things went between them. That's the thing about traveling, isn't it? The secrets just stay behind. No mention need be made.

She slowly drifts off to sleep with images of flowers and palms in her head. Throughout the night the oil-dampened wick flickers away beside her, silent as a dream.

Chapter 21

Smoke

Even the lowest whisper can sound like a shout if it carries the words one has waited to hear.

"I believe I have seen exactly what it is that you've been looking for."

The words are spoken in a low tone, from the mouth of Chen Lu to the ear of Devlin Richards. But Richards looks puzzled by the statement. He quietly cuts the tip off a fresh cigar and tosses it on the floor. The two men flank a carved wooden Indian that stands just inside a large bay window. The white letters along the base of the statue read "Jake's Tobacco Hall." The curved copper shell of the window, patina-green with age, covers the whole front of the shop and thrusts out so far onto the sidewalk that pedestrians have to walk around it. The bay holds several armchairs and foot stools and is a favorite spot for men in the neighborhood to gather for an afternoon cigar. But this morning, the big window is nearly empty.

The sweet smell of whiskey-soaked tobacco fills the air. Sunlight warms the shoulders of Devlin and Chen Lu as they lurk near the glass. Devlin looks at the Chinaman, waiting for more information. He impatiently thrusts the cigar in his mouth but doesn't yet light it.

"Information from the shipwreck is what you desire, no?" Chen Lu smiles. "Is that not what you came to me looking for many days ago?"

"Maybe."

"Information is what I have. And more."

Devlin shrugs. "Looks like a lot of different stuff has turned up from that ship. Most of it has turned out to be trash. You'll need something pretty good to hold my attention longer than it takes me to smoke this."

Chen Lu nods. "Perhaps you are correct." Devlin finds the man's smile irritating.

The waiting continues. Devlin finally walks to the end of the counter and lights his cigar from a small gas flame that dances atop a brass fixture shaped like a naked woman. Returning to the bay window, he blows smoke at the Chinese merchant, who closes his eyes.

"Say your piece, old man. I'm tired of your teasing."

Chen Lu speaks in carefully measured tones. "You are looking for the belongings of a specific man on that ship. He was a passenger, no? Not part of the crew."

Devlin nods slightly. "And how do you know this?"

"I have heard the whispers from the same sailors as you. Men come and go from my shop. Import and export is my business. Mine is a place where they can sell the things they have brought home with them. Ivory. Jewelry. Exotic sculptures. When they come to me,

I talk. I have heard the same stories as you. That this man carried something. Exactly what, I have no certainty."

Devlin blows another smoke puff, this time toward the window, watching the smoke cling to and cloud the already grimy glass. "Yeah? Well, I've come to believe that whatever that man carried, if he carried anything at all, went right to the bottom along with the ship. Every trail we have followed has come up empty."

"We?" Chen Lu says with raised eyebrows.

"I'm working for someone on this. Getting paid. You think I'd waste time chasing down this dead end on my own time?"

"What is it, do you think, that this person seeks?"

"I'm not sure," Devlin lies. "Guy was a scientist, so they must be looking for some piece of science equipment. Probably worthless to most people, unless you know what to do with it."

"Where was the ship coming from?"

"From right here in Boston. Heading to Liverpool."

Chen Lu laughs. "There has been talk of diamonds and gold. And fools believe it."

"Even if anything did survive, it was picked over by whoever found it on the beach." Devlin shrugs. "Not very likely that anything is going to make its way up from the Cape and into your shop. You might end up with some trinkets, I suppose. But the real prize, if there even was one, is long gone."

Chen Lu nods. "Perhaps you are correct. But still you seek. And you talk to me."

Devlin Richards nods. "So what is it that you do have to offer? What is your information, exactly?"

"Just that people have come in, selling what they have found. Some brass. Cheap jewelry. Personal effects."

"Why would you think I'd be interested in knowing this?"

"Because I have other items on their way," Chen Lu states. "One man even told me he will bring in a box of some sort. I have not seen it yet." He watches Devlin's reaction carefully. "Just wanted to judge your interest level before deciding whether to buy it from him."

Devlin leans forward, obviously intrigued. "I guess I'd be interested in seeing it. Can't promise any more than that."

"I understand."

"When do you think this man will visit your shop?"

"I can't say really. It was just a general statement that he may stop by. It's my understanding that he does not actually own the box himself. So there may be even more people involved. When I know more, you will know more."

Chen Lu pulls a Manchurian-style pipe from his inside coat pocket and tugs at its telescoping stem. He packs the silver bowel with tobacco and holds its jade mouthpiece in his teeth. He and Devlin smoke silently for the next five minutes, both lost in their own thoughts.

Chapter 22

Currents

A comfortable mentorship travels on a collision course with a spouse's circumspection.

Jonathan Morgan agrees to take Amanda to the Asian Antique Emporium on the morning of July 3rd, and they plan to show the box to the old man who runs the place. Amanda intends only to ask him for advice on how to open more of its levels. Fascinated by the whole idea of such boxes, Jonathan also plans to browse the collection of other boxes in the shop. He may buy one for himself.

But as they hitch up his wagon and climb aboard, Beverly appears from out of nowhere, casting a chastising glance at the old man for accompanying this separated woman through town without an escort. The old woman tells him coolly that he needs to help her with something in the house today, and asks if it wouldn't be better for someone else to take Amanda to the store. Jonathan steps down silently and slinks over to Jasper's house. He stands under the small portico for a moment, knocks, then disappears into the gap of the tall front door.

While she waits, Amanda decides to run back inside for a moment, half to avoid Beverly's gaze, but also to retrieve some of the silverware she's been storing in her suitcase. If she's going to make a transition away from the Morgans' house, she'll need a cash stake in order to do so. Perhaps she can sell some pieces of silver at the shop. Sorting through the rolled cloth she keeps under the bed, she takes only some spare spoons. She doesn't yet want to break up the matched table settings, figuring they'll be worth more together.

Jonathan returns with Jasper, stating in a businesslike voice that Jasper has agreed to take Amanda to the shop. They'll stop by and pick up Charles along the way. Jasper climbs aboard, greeting Amanda with a smile and insisting he always enjoys visiting the Asian Antiques Emporium just to see its exotic wares.

Soon they are out of the neighborhood and traveling down Hanover Street, with a quick stop at Clark Street to drag Charles along with them. Amada sits in awkward silence, wondering what the men must think about Jonathan's absence. The reality of what it means to be a separated woman is slowly creeping into her daily life. People really do view such women with suspicion. Her social standing may be nil, but these two, thankfully, remain gentlemen. Any reservations they may have about her perceived impropriety remain unspoken.

Amanda decides to break the silence, saying something, anything, to clear the air.

"Have … um … either of you heard of someone named Tesla?"

The men look at each other for a moment, not sure how to respond.

"Is this someone local?" Jasper asks.

"I don't know. I don't think so. It's a name that's mentioned a few times in the diary I'm reading—the one that I found in this box. At first I thought Tesla was the name of some woman he knew. But as I've read more, I've come to realize that it's the name of a man he worked for. The way he talks about this Tesla person, it seems that a lot of people must know him."

Jasper strokes his chin for a moment. "Can't say as it rings a bell."

Charles looks more optimistic. "Well, as someone familiar with engineering and technical publications, I can tell you that there is a fairly well-known inventor named Tesla. His full name is Nikola Tesla, I believe. Has something to do with electricity. A few years ago my nephew, who is involved in electrical work, used to mention his name quite often."

Amanda sits forward, her excitement growing. "Yes! That would make sense. The gentleman who owned the diary, Mr. Victor Marius, was an electrical engineer. So maybe he would have known another electrical engineer!"

"Okay then, yes," says Charles. "I guess I do sort of know who Tesla is. Raymond was just out of high school and looking for work, and he was hired to work on a project over in Great Barrington, Massachusetts. It was probably a good, oh, maybe five years ago. They lit up a whole big building over there, dozens and dozens of light bulbs and wires running everywhere. Raymond was hired as unskilled labor at the time, just to drill holes and pull wires. But he sure did make a big deal out of what they were doing. It wasn't the first building in the country to be lit up by electric lights, but it may have been the largest installation ever. Raymond said there was something really special about the project."

"Yes," Jasper nods. "I do remember reading something about that. There was something different about the way they produced the electricity that made it a sort of milestone."

Charles shifts in his seat, like he's suddenly excited about the topic and bursting with news. Amanda begins to relax, glad she was able to pick a topic that helped make the three of them more comfortable and talkative.

"Well," Charles explains, "from what I know of it, there are two completely different ways of producing and distributing electricity.

One's called *direct* and the other's *alternating*. Most of the first installations of electric lights in this country used direct current."

He moves his hand in a wide circle. "Now, direct current power once it's produced by a generator, flows through wires just like water flows through a water pipe. Just travels in one direction. Of course the pipe has to be a complete loop in order for it to work. Whatever is hooked to the 'pipe' takes energy from the electricity that's passing through. The more lights you hook to it, the more electricity is used up. Eventually the lights grow dimmer when there are just too many of them."

They turn a corner onto Cross Street. A fruit vender catches Amanda's eye and winks at her. She smiles, but looks away. The street turns into a bumpy cobblestone ride. They all brace themselves against the bouncing and jostling.

"I think that project on which my nephew worked was the first big public example of the other way of doing it—of alternating current. The way he explained it, if DC current is like a looping pipe, AC is more like a long chain that moves back and forth." Charles moves his hand through the air like a saw to explain the concept while his other hand grasps the wooden seat to steady himself.

"It's still like a big loop, but inside the wire, the electricity shifts back and forth tremendously fast. There are two big advantages to that. First, you can plug as many lights into the system as you need. The difference is that you just make the alternating chain work harder, and if you're successful, all the lights still burn at the same brightness."

"Sounds like hooey to me," Jasper snorts.

"Yeah, well, I'm probably not explaining it correctly. But that's the general idea of it."

"So what's the second advantage?" Amanda asks, determined to keep the conversation going.

"The real benefit is that alternating current can be transmitted across long distances. A central generator can light up a whole city if it's powerful enough. Raymond said direct current can't do that. It loses its power with distance. With DC, you'd have to place generators in every neighborhood. It makes an electrical system sprawling and complicated."

Charles realizes he's rambling and quickly returns to his story. "So, anyway, when the Great Barrington project happened, a whole bunch of engineers and politicians came out to watch them throw the switch because they wanted to see a major test of an AC installation. It was a fairly big deal at the time."

"So what did this Mr. Tesla have to do with it?" Amanda asks.

"I don't really know. Raymond just told me Tesla was there and that he was involved. He's a bit of an eccentric, I hear, and apparently he's a bitter rival of the illustrious inventor Thomas Edison. I guess he has nothing but bad things to say about Edison."

They all breathe a sigh of relief as they finally turn off the bumpy street and onto Sudbury Street along the edge of the Commons. The day is warm, and several couples can be seen strolling along the paths.

"Really? I ... I'm surprised," Amanda says. "Mr. Edison seems like ... well, such a bright man. A friend of mine on the Cape had an Edison phonograph. The one with the spinning wax cylinders. I used to love to listen to it."

Charles nods. "Yes, of course. Edison's a great man. I have one of his phonographs myself. But to hear Raymond tell it, Edison, even today, remains convinced that direct current will rule the world. He's *determined* that it will, actually. Tesla, apparently, is an alternating-current champion. But since he's the less well known of the two, and since he has a lot less funding, he probably has a big uphill battle on his hands. My guess is that he was at the Great Barrington event because he knew it was a big deal."

"So that's where Tesla and Edison disagree?" Amanda asks. "Over the two types of electrical current?"

"That, plus Tesla claims that Edison cheated him," Charles laughs. "My nephew says Tesla was always grumbling about that. I'm not sure what it was all about, but I can tell you that after helping with the project, Raymond was totally smitten with the concept of alternating current. He ended up getting a job with the company called Westinghouse that made the new AC generators. I hear from him every Christmas. He's somewhere near Pittsburgh. He likes to make all these marvelous prognostications about the future. I tell you, he makes me laugh, that boy."

Amanda is fascinated. "Does your nephew still work with this Mr. Tesla?"

"I don't know. I'm not sure if Tesla is still associated with the company or not."

Amanda nods, then sits back in contemplation. Maybe she should try to contact his nephew Raymond. Perhaps that would be a way to find out more about Tesla.

Maybe she could even ask if he, or anyone at the factory, knew who Victor Marius was, and why he was on the boat.

Chapter 23

Tesla

"Problems continue with Pearl Street Station."

Nikola Tesla reads the headline on his newspaper and chuckles to himself. Of course they're having problems with that, and with every other station that Edison has built in New York. Whenever they add a new home or business to one of those circuits, the performance of all the other customers degrades. How delightful!

"Success," Tesla mutters smugly, "ends up being the enemy for that bastard Edison. Every new customer is one more nail in the coffin of his technology."

The scientist exits his new lab and flips off the power switch to one of his experiments. He then locks the front door and walks two blocks to the nearest telegraph station. He's actually having a telephone installed in his lab next week, but he's not sure if the expense is worth it. So few acquaintances have telephones that he doesn't really have anyone to call.

For now, telegraph is still his best communication option.

"Good afternoon, Mr. Tesla!" the man behind the Western Union counter calls out. In the past few days the engineer has become one of his best customers.

"Yes, yes. Hello Irving. How are you?" Tesla's thick Serbian accent is tough to decipher.

"Can't complain at all, sir. Beautiful day. There's been a trickle of customers."

Tesla nods and picks up a telegram form.

"Another long one today, sir?"

"Yes, indeed. When are you going to start giving discounts for telegrams over fifty words?"

The operator laughs. "Can't do that, sir. In fact, I should charge extra. My hand gets pretty tired after twenty-five or so."

Tesla laughs, but in his mind he quickly pictures a machine that could be used to automate telegraphs. It would have a keyboard of about 200 or so of the most common words. Just pressing one of the keys would automatically send the proper dot and dash impulses associated with that word. The operator would have to manually send only the more unusual words. Eventually such a machine could be improved upon, to the point where an operator isn't needed at all.

He shakes his head, forcing the image from his mind. He knows there is no way he could ever build all the machines that he dreams up. It's distracting to him when such thoughts linger too long. Besides, why build a machine for a technology that could eventually be replaced by the budding telephone system? Many an engineer has wasted his time developing solutions for problems that were abruptly solved by others.

"Where are you sending this one, sir?" the telegraph operator asks as Tesla scribbles. "To Pittsburgh again?"

"Indeed I am!"

The operator waits until Tesla looks like he's finished with his writing, then clicks his keys to get Pittsburgh on the line. "How many words?"

"Well, let's see." He runs his finger along the lines.

"I'd say about eighty-five or so. Depends on if you want to include the *and*s and the *or*s."

"I always do, sir! You know that!" He chuckles as he takes the beige paper. "You're determined to wear out my tapping finger!"

Irving the telegraph operator starts to tap out the message. It's meant for George Westinghouse himself. The telegram starts with a little joke about the problems Edison is encountering with his New York installations, then moves on to a brief description of Tesla's evolving plans for the power plant he's designing for the Chicago Columbia Exhibition scheduled for next year. Preliminary plans will be sent within the month, he promises.

He finishes up with a brief description of some of his radio experiments and laments that he can't get Westinghouse to raise his interest level in the technology. But he promises that his personal radio experiments won't get in the way of his work for the all-important Chicago project.

"Fascinating," says Irving. "I learn so much about communications just by sending your telegraphs!"

Tesla smiles.

"What's the Columbia Exhibition?"

Tesla asks Irving if he remembers the American Centennial exhibition of 1876.

"I was pretty young then, sir. But I've certainly heard people talk about it."

Tesla explains that this will be even larger and grander. He then tells the young man about the electricity. The whole exhibition will be electrified, with lights and maybe even some motors.

"I wish I could go. I really do."

"Well, when we build it, we'll need help. Maybe I'll keep you in mind."

"Really? Would you do that?"

Tesla winks. "Depends. I certainly remember who's been nice to me. And I really do get sick of paying for all these short words in my telegrams."

They both laugh, and Tesla heads back up the street, toward his combination apartment and lab.

Rather than turning the power back on for his lab experiments, he turns to a large notebook. The idea for the telegraph machine stoked some ideas, not for the machine itself, but for some other concepts he's had since returning to New York.

He flips to the page in the notebook that reads "Global Wireless Communications." Beneath this he's already sketched a tall tower that looks like a wire-frame mushroom. At the bottom of the page, he starts to write. As he does so, he gets a glazed look in his eyes. The words devolve into broken English as he writes faster. He tells about voices, pictures, radio waves that fly like birds. Images that move.

"And even the electricity itself doesn't need wires!" he scrawls. "I can send it where I want, when I want. I can control it all!"

His hands shake as he continues to write, and his hand eventually cramps as he finishes nearly eight more pages of sloppy notes with a labyrinthine of sketches that don't quite lead anywhere.

At least, not to anyone but him.

Chapter 24

Orient Expressions

The shop of Chen Lu is immaculate. Amanda can't spot a speck of dust anywhere. The crystal gleams. The watercolor paintings look fresh, like they were just painted yesterday. The furniture, what there is of it, looks exotic and flawless. Reddish stained wood. Round brass plates shining in the middle of doors and on curling side handles. Even the keyholes in some of the drawer fronts look new and strangely mysterious.

Along the far side of the shop, she sees a section of shelves that hold jade, carved ivory, and several puzzle boxes. There must be a dozen of them. Some are very plain while a couple appear to be even more ornate than the one she holds.

As she and the two men walk down the length of the shop, it occurs to her that Mr. Lu isn't just a dealer in art and curiosities; he is also an expert at restoring things to their original state. She feels better now about making the trip. If he does know something about puzzle boxes, at the very least, perhaps he could help her fix the broken piece.

Near the rear of the shop, she sees two people, an older Chinese man and a well-dressed white woman looking at a selection of amber pins spread out atop a glass countertop. The man turns and nods at them as they enter. He tells the woman he will be right back.

The shopkeeper is about sixty years old, with gray hair pulled back in a neat braid. His mustache is thin, with a wisp of longer whiskers on each side hanging to the bottom of his chin. His coat is green with a slightly darker pattern of green woven through the silk. Charles steps forward in greeting. He and Chen Lu exchange pleasantries, then Charles explains to the shopkeeper that he's not bringing him any train station lost-and-found items this time. Instead he has brought an acquaintance (he gestures to Amanda) with an interesting puzzle box. Would he mind taking a look?

"Of course, of course," Chen Lu smiles. "No interesting boxes have come into the shop for several weeks."

Amanda steps forward as Charles introduces her, offering the box for inspection like a Magi's gift. The old man lifts it from her hands, and she clasps her fingers together, leaning forward slightly, attentive as a mother with a sick child.

Chen Lu is silent, turning the box over and over. His eyes widen a bit as he studies its height. "You get this where? Most interesting!"

"I found it," Amanda says, then immediately wonders if she should have concocted a different story. She has no idea if she can trust this man who has such a keen interest in boxes and toys.

He rattles the box, smiles, then sits in a straight-backed chair. "I recognize style. This box probably eight, maybe ten years old. Manufactured in Japan, and sold all over Asia and the Orient." Amanda decides that the old man's English is fairly good, but his accent is thick. She has to listen carefully to follow what he's saying.

Chen Lu smiles for a second, then adds, "Maybe not correct to say 'all over.' Plenty of similar boxes around. But I think no more than 300 of this type model produced. I talk to other collectors. These are made by company that also makes playing cards. First boxes were created to hold their cards. When people start buying the card sets just because they like the puzzles, the company started making

147

the boxes alone—moving toward fancier ones. Harder-to-open ones."

Chen Lu strokes the wooden diamond on the box front. "This box is type from the end of that era, just before they switched to making other types of games. Board games. Pull toys. These were made mostly for export just like the card games. They sent to China, Siam, Korea, maybe Southern Russia too. They tended to show up in popular port cities where trade ships go. Just popular curiosities that visitors might take home. Maybe rare, but not so rare that boxes become all that highly valued. Understand?"

He chuckles and points to the shelves. "I have luck offering them in my shop here when I find them, but I don't consider them valuable. Just toys."

He examines the box for a moment, then, in the fastest series of moves that Amanda has ever seen, he opens the various levels. With intimate familiarity, he even finds the little section that needs to be pinched, just like Jasper showed her. But then he hesitates.

"I had thought this was standard diamond model. But maybe I am wrong? This one seems different, no?"

Jasper nods. "Yes. It's been modified."

Chen Lu looks at the base of the unit, squinting at the teak. "Do you know why?"

Jasper shakes his head. "I don't know. But it does seem fancy. This one has teak and that ... well, whatever that other wood is."

The old man looks closely. "Katsura maybe. And some maple, Japanese maple." Chen Lu smiles. Amanda sees something in his eyes as he looks at the lower part of the box. She's not sure exactly what it is, but she's seen it before ... in the eyes of horses waiting at the door of their stalls. Or a dog waiting to eat. She swallows a bit as the old man continues.

148

"Yes, you are right. Original builders probably would not have used the teak. Look here. Transition between the woods is awkward. The hand which added this lower part? Seems less skilled than the original craftsman."

The other men nod. Amanda's heart races. She realizes that the sailor, or engineer, or whatever Victor was must have added it himself. If fits with what little she knows about him. He needed more. More space. Bigger projects. More places to store and save and grow. It was like he had dozens of important things to say and do. And the box, where he decided to keep his most important things, just couldn't contain all his hopes and ambitions. He added to it. More than once.

She fights the impulse to take the box back, to close it up and hide Victor's world from their prying eyes. She feels protective and slightly hurt by the comment that his addition was of a less skillful application of the craft.

Chen Lu pinches and bends the top edge of the inside compartment, releasing the panel and spinning it free. He notices the flapping drawer front.

"That's … that's part of the reason we're here," Amanda says, distracting herself from her swirl of thoughts. "Can you … can you fix it? And can you help us open the other levels without breaking anything else?"

She sees him hesitate. "I … I'm not sure. I might be able. But I need to give this some thought." He looks toward the back of his shop. "Why don't you leave it here for a couple days? I will try to open the various levels as time allows."

She shakes her head no.

"Would you be interested in simply selling the box as it is?"

She bites her tongue and looks at the floor.

"How much are you offering?" Jasper asks the Chinaman.

"How much do you want for it?" Chen Lu speaks directly to Amanda, ignoring the men.

"It's not for sale," she replies quickly. "I only want to get it repaired, and maybe to get some help opening the rest of the levels."

"Yes. Of course. You must leave it here for that."

"I ... I had hoped to watch. To see how you do it."

The old man taps his foot and looks at the regulator clock on the wall.

"You should sell it. You get nice financial gain from what you found. Surely everything has its price, no?"

"Why don't you make her an offer then?" Charles laughs. "Like Jasper just said?"

"Indeed." The shopkeeper nods. "Perhaps yes. How does six dollars sound?"

"No. It's not for sale."

"No? Well, I suppose I could go as high as ten dollars. But that's it."

She shakes her head.

"Fifteen!"

"I'm sorry." Amanda reaches for the box. She feels increasingly uncomfortable here.

Suddenly the shopkeeper blurts out an offer of fifty-five dollars.

"Take it!" Jasper encourages. "My God, that's more than many people make in a month!"

"I'm sorry. It's just … I can't."

Near the back of the shop, a woman's voice calls out. She has made her selection from the array of amber jewelry and would like to talk to the shopkeeper about holding it for her until tomorrow. He holds up a finger, urging her to wait a moment.

Charles scratches his chin for a moment, then looks at the shopkeeper. "Hey, why is this so valuable to you? For God's sake, it's just a puzzle. You even said yourself they're not so rare. I mean … I can buy a decent horse for fifty-five dollars!"

"This one … it is … different enough. I can resell it for a bit more, that's all."

Charles squints. "Last time I checked the prices on your puzzle boxes they were all under ten dollars."

Chen Lu reluctantly hands the box back to Amanda. "All the more reason to take good offer when given. Second chance not to come again."

She grasps the box tightly to her chest. "I'm sorry." She looks him in the eye. "So … what of the repairs? And the help? Can you still do that?"

"It will cost money. At least thirty dollars."

The men look at each other. "Oh come now!" Charles blurts out. "That's absurd!"

"Little time available these days. Very busy." The shopkeeper stands. Some sand has seeped from the box and has fallen on his clothes. He brushes it away.

"Come on, dear," Charles says. "I know you like that thing, but you really ought to just sell it to him."

But Amanda just looks at the floor. Perhaps the silverware? She quickly pulls the pieces out of her coat, grateful to be able to change the subject. "What about these?"

Chen Lu studies them, remarks favorably on their quality, and offers her thirteen dollars for the lot, which she gladly accepts.

"Thank you for your time, sir," Jasper says.

Chun Lu nods and the trio makes their way toward the door. Amanda looks back before they leave and sees the old man's gaze following the box.

"One thing more," he calls out. "Be careful when you open the rest of the compartments!"

"Why is that?" asks Charles.

"I hear stories. Not common. But stories. Like booby traps. Things may be inside such boxes. Hidden knives or explosives."

"That's ancient history," Charles calls back. "That sort of thing is just for big treasure boxes in palaces. Kings and stuff. Years and years ago."

Chun Lu nods. "Perhaps. One never knows. And you have a box that is larger than some, no?" His high-pitched laughter fills the air as they exit to the street.

They climb back into the wagon, with Charles muttering something about foolishness. They ride in silence for several minutes, Amanda gazing into the windows of passing stores.

The fifty-five dollars would go a long way for a woman in her situation. She knows it, and understands that that these men know it too. The Morgans are quite charitable toward her. But she's overstaying her welcome, and that money would have helped her move on from their home.

152

Back in the shop, Chen Lu finishes with his jewelry buyer and calls out toward the rear of the building. A pale man with sunken eyes parts the red doorway curtain, slinking slowly forward. His steps are plodding, as if he's walking in a stupor. The smell of burnt opium trails behind him. Chen Lu smiles at the man. He holds another white packet in front of him like a prize. The sullen man looks at it longingly.

Chen Lu nods toward the road.

"That wagon that just left. Follow it. Tell me where they go. If they go to other shops, keep following it until they go back home. Tell me where that home is. Tell me where that woman lives. Tell me if she still has her wooden box with her. Do you understand?"

The man reaches for the packet. Chen Lu snaps his hand away and places it in his own pocket. "No. Do this first. Then you get your hop. Maybe you even get more than this if the information is good."

Chen Lu reaches behind one of the counters and produces a battered Kodak camera, then rummages around for a roll of Eastman American Film. He steps into the dark back room and quickly loads the camera. "Take this with you. I want photos of all of those people. But don't let them see you."

The man grabs the camera, and his steps suddenly quicken. He heads for the door, catching sight of the wagon just as it rounds a distant street corner.

The shopkeeper hurries back through the same red curtain, widening his eyes to adjust to the dim light. He sees another man sitting at a small table, cleaning his fingernails with a knife.

"You!" Chen Lu says accusingly. "You gave him smoke, didn't you! In here! I told you that no one is to smoke in here!"

The man looks up, his face slowly coming into view through the smoky haze as Chen Lu's eyes adjust. It's the face of Devlin Richards. "Relax old man. It's business. Same reason you're eventually going to give him more hop. We all need a little help now and then."

"Many paintings here. And cloth. It is not allowed to smoke in here!"

Devlin gives him an irate look. The old man pulls out a chair and sits, sweeping aside a small bit of spilled powder.

"All of this aside," Chen Lu continues, "I may have brand-new information on the article you seek. The one you mentioned yesterday? I will know even more in due time."

Devlin stops cleaning his nails and waves the knife at Chen Lu. "What do you mean? What do you know?"

The shopkeeper smiles, deliberately slowing his voice, enjoying the power of making this angry, volatile man wait for the information. "Oh, I'm not certain yet. I just may have some new details. Time will tell."

"If you know something—" Devlin jams the knife point-first into the tabletop. "I want to know what it is."

Chen Lu eyes him coolly. "You want information, you let me collect it the right way. We do not need to scare anyone away."

"What is it that you think you have, old man?"

"I don't know yet. But as I say, it might be important to you. I suggest you proceed as if it is indeed the information you seek."

Devlin snatches the knife back. "Meaning?"

"Meaning I don't expect threats from you. And you know what happened to the last man who threatened me."

The southerner growls, "I should cut you right now, old man. I really should."

"Business ...," Chen Lu whispers, holding Devlin's gaze.

Devlin squints, then nods, putting his knife away. "Fair enough. Business. But that information better be damn good." He rises and heads out the back door, squinting at the sunlight.

Up the road, Amanda finds herself gripping her skirt with nervous, angry hands as they ride. It's a habit she proudly stopped after she left Wayne, but it still comes out now and then when she feels stressed.

Finally Jasper breaks the silence. "You know what I think?"

"No sir. What?"

"I think you're sweet on him."

"What? On ... on who?" Her mind races. *Does he mean Jonathan? Mr. Morgan? How could he think that? How could he even—*

"Sweet on that sailor! The one who owned the box. You've sorted through all the silly things he collected. You've read his diary."

Her eyes widen, large enough that the light from the sunny day suddenly makes them ache. "What? Why that ... that's ridiculous. How can you say something like that?"

"I don't know," Jasper laughs. He's driving the wagon now and he flicks the reins to hurry the horse through an intersection ahead of an approaching streetcar. "Just a feeling, I guess."

"Well, I think it's a silly feeling. I mean, he's dead Mr. Stokes. I think that's a very morbid thought."

Jasper shrugs. "Well, perhaps you're right. Perhaps it is silly." They ride in silence for another minute. "So why are you keeping the box then?"

She doesn't answer.

"Think it's worth more than what he offered?"

"I don't know. It doesn't matter. It means something to me is all." She wonders how she can explain it, or even if she should. "It's … I don't know. It's like my last connection to my old life. Something I found right at the end of it all, right before I left Cape Cod."

"And those silver spoons? Weren't they part of your old life too?"

"Those are different. Those are part of the old life that I'd rather forget."

She says nothing for the rest of the ride. All three of them are oblivious to a disheveled man who follows them on foot, hanging back a few hundred feet. The slow Boston traffic makes it possible for him to keep up with the horses.

Amanda finds herself anxious to get home, and to return the diary to its place of safety.

But the accusation continues to bother her. Sweet on a dead man? Sweet on someone she has never met? The very idea is absurd. Her interest is purely analytical. Historic. Plus, she thinks maybe, just maybe, hidden somewhere in that diary there might be instructions on how to open the rest of the box. The thought of booby traps scares her a bit, but she's still willing to proceed. But first she wants to read some more, and see what Victor has to say about this.

Chapter 25

Independence Day

July 4, 1891

Amanda rises at 7:00 a.m. Three hours pass before she realizes the day is a holiday. The gentle reminder comes from the Morgans as she shares her plans to walk to some shops to look for work.

"Goodness, dear, I don't know if they'll be open!" says Beverly. "It's the Fourth of July after all."

The young woman laughs and rethinks her plans. *The Fourth of July?* She knew the date was lurking. She just didn't realize it was today. Other than sunrises and sunsets, she's lost all track of time lately. Her mind is a fog of plans and worries.

Electing to enjoy the holiday, she takes a different sort of walk, following the same route she took with Jasper and Charles the day before. The stroll takes her over a dozen blocks, toward the Boston Commons and through that park, on into the Boston Public Garden. It feels good just to enjoy the open spaces. To smell the flower beds. To merge into the holiday crowd and to be one with it.

In spite of the hot day, Amanda sees many women in their full finery—bustles with short trains dragging close behind like wrinkled ducklings.

Amanda's dress is plain and straight. The fabric is light, more suitable for a sunny day. She marvels at the dresses and their yards of trailing fabric, but realizes that many of the modern bustles lack a certain presence. When she was younger, the rear of a dress was much more pronounced. Now the bustles have faded to little more than a pad over a woman's posterior, covered with a pitiable amount of cloth that barely hangs to the ground. Just the hint of a train. Why even bother?

Women look more like their real selves now. But modern modification of the female form is far from over. She can see that the most fashionable young girls, the ones with the latest shorter hair and the finest light summer dresses, are also experimenting with severe corsets that seem to make their waists impossibly thin.

Amanda has owned only two fine bustled dresses in her life. Since she is blessed with a thin waist, she's never needed a corset, but now wonders how she'd look with everything tucked in tight in one of those severe bustiers. Too many curves, she decides. Too much to reveal.

A man with a large handlebar mustache and a bowler hat whizzes by her. He suddenly curves, like he's gliding on air, and heads back toward her on the park's wide sidewalk.

"Good day, madam!" he declares, lifting his hat. He still glides, effortlessly looping around her.

"Gracious, how do you do that?" she asks.

"Do what? This?" He lifts one leg high and continues to curve around her in a small circle.

She looks at his feet. He rides along with a foot-high wheel strapped to each ankle. He bows his legs slightly outward to transfer the weight to each wheel. They're known as bicycle skates and include a small stirrup for each foot.

"May I have this dance?" he jokes, pirouetting in place right in front of her.

"I think not. I don't think I could keep up with you."

"Suit yourself." He winks, pressing the bowler back down onto his head. With a few muscular pumps, he whizzes on up the street toward the main entrance of the Public Garden.

Continuing on her walk, Amanda enters the heart of the Public Garden and walks among the flowers and the curving pond. Someone has set up a large telescope near the pathway. It sits atop a broad tripod and includes a brass barrel that's nearly as long as a telegraph pole. It gleams, scepter-like, in the sun.

Because it's daytime, Amanda guesses at first that the scope must be pointed at some distant landmark, but it's positioned too high. She realizes it's pointed at the daytime moon. A man with a straw hat, mustache, and wire-frame glasses collects nickels and allows people to gaze through the eyepiece.

She pays him five cents and joins a short line. "The moon is constantly in motion," the Telescope Man explains to the crowd, "so I must constantly adjust the huge scope to keep the half crescent within view." He does this with a couple knobs on the side of the tripod. When it's her turn, Amanda looks through the lens and sees nothing but bright white. Perhaps nighttime viewing would have been a better choice.

"On the eyepiece!" the man says. "Adjust that little ring and it will bring everything into focus."

With a few twists she suddenly can see the moon's rough surface quite clearly. It's like looking at the top of a cake or a massive sandcastle. There are sharp shadows stretching out from the mountainous craters. There are stark whites and dull grays. So much detail, yet it seems like a forsaken desert.

"My," she comments, "the shadows are so crisp and sharp!"

"Scientists don't believe there's any atmosphere on the moon," the proprietor says. "No clouds or fog to filter the sun's rays. It's blindingly bright and clear up there!"

She takes in the beautiful, desolate panorama, finding it both troubling and strangely soothing. She stares until the moon slowly arcs out of view and people behind her start to grumble. As she steps back, the Telescope Man quickly adjusts the knobs and the next customer steps up to the eyepiece.

"I had no idea that the moon moves so fast!" she says.

"Yes, indeed," the Telescope Man smiles. "Constant motion. The universe never sleeps."

Amanda's holiday lunch is little more than bread and an apple, eaten while watching a puppet show. She leaves before the performance ends. The children's laughter, usually so charming to her ears, seems like fingernails on a chalkboard today. The feeling troubles her as she walks away. Before leaving Wayne, she had very much expected to be a doting mother. But now, who knows?

She wanders aimlessly for a while, arriving back home in the late afternoon. She carries a small container of strawberries purchased at a fruit stand. She dines quietly with the Morgans. As they clear the table, they invite her to accompany them to a fireworks display to be held down by the Charles River.

"Those shows always scare the life out of me," Beverly laments, right hand pressed to her chest, "but Jonathan always insists that we go."

Amanda declines politely, and Beverly doesn't seem to mind. A growing coolness lurks between them.

Amanda justifies her avoidance by telling herself that she needs to get a good night's sleep. She can attack her job hunt again in the morning. Bidding the Morgans good evening, she picks up the remaining strawberries and climbs the stairs to her room.

The evening is warm and the bed chamber oppressively hot. Instead of undressing, she opens the window and climbs out onto the low roof, the space where she earlier had watched the pigeons gather.

With a slow, groaning, after-dinner stretch, she takes in the view, looking over adjacent rooftops.

Across the alley, the houses are slightly lower, and she can see far beyond them. There's even a patch of ocean-blue water in the distance.

The evening air is sweet. She paces around the roofline like the edges of a cage. Amanda understands now that she will not end up renting a room from the Morgans on a long-term basis. But if she did, she might have asked them for permission to turn this space into a summer sleeping porch—just a screened-in section with a small cot—a great way to escape the interior humidity. But tonight she will sleep inside, enduring the heat and the flies with a soothing wet washcloth on her forehead.

Amanda settles down on the tin roof and stares lazily at the puffy clouds. She munches on the strawberries while vaguely making plans for the following day.

A slight grin creeps across her face. No matter what sort of problems a person might face, most of them can be erased, at least for a few moments, by the yellow light of a warm summer evening and the taste of fresh strawberries.

A distant melody catches her ear. At first it's little more than background music to her thoughts. But it slowly grows louder. There's also shouting, clapping, and laughter. Sitting up, she brushes green strawberry tops toward the edge of the roof and listens more intently. Yes, she really does hear music. There are strains from a fiddle and maybe a piano. The clapping is done in time with the rhythm.

At first it seems the sounds are wafting forth from the open windows of the house across the alley. But as she walks to the edge of the roof, she realizes it comes from just beyond the row of houses. About a block away she sees the top of what must be a large barn or a carriage house.

Mariner's House.

Isn't that the name of a building that's located in that direction? It's a large rooming house, and the barn must sit behind it.

Amanda has never been to Mariner's House, but everyone in the neighborhood knows what the place is for. It sits just off North Square, an easy five-minute walk from the waterfront. People welcome the sailors who stay there, but whisper to their daughters to steer clear of them.

Mariner's House itself is an imposing structure. Built forty-some years ago, it's halfway between a house and a building, with more than a dozen rooms to rent inside. Some of the bedrooms contain multiple beds. It's far from private, but bunk beds are still a luxury to sailors who are used to sleeping in cramped berths or shipboard hammocks.

It's a sprightly melody, and Amanda recognizes the song. From this far away she can't hear all of it, but it stokes a childhood memory. *Betsy from Pike?* Before his disappearance, her father and his friends used to sing that one. Her parents liked barn dances too. They used to bring her along. She would sit in the hayloft with other

162

children, looking down at the swirling crowd through warm evening air filled with smoke, music, and the smell of spilled beer. From the musicians on the stage, she would hear Italian accents and Irish brogues. Those voices would warp the choruses to the point where she couldn't always understand the words. But the music still warmed her. She would lose herself in it. Sometimes groups of children would climb down from the loft and join the dance. Amanda would spin until her energy waned. She'd eventually fall asleep on a pile of rope or maybe a hay bale until strong arms lifted her and carried her back home.

Such a happy part of her past.

Despite her promise to get a good night's sleep, the fiddle playing is a siren's call. Back into her room. Amanda changes into a clean, loose-fitting dress and a comfortable pair of shoes. She rushes down the stairs, unsure exactly what she's doing or why. But she wants to listen and she wants to see.

Chapter 26

Her

Mariner's House is a place where sailors can get away from their ship for a while, get a good meal, go to church, meet other sailors, and trade stories, job leads, and laments about their chosen profession.

New ships in port. New captains looking for help. There's always news to share around the house's huge oak table every morning.

The local sailors association sometimes rents the barn behind the building and uses it as an informal meeting hall. It also sponsors occasional dances on Saturdays or holidays.

While no alcohol is served, it always finds its way to the perimeter. Bottles of beer are stashed in a nearby creek. Whiskey bottles are shoved into pockets. Cigarettes and fistfights lurk in the back alley along with drunken sailors urinating on the bushes.

But the dances themselves provide a wholesome outlet for a group of men who don't have much money or social opportunities. Local woman who dare to join the ruckus are always welcomed by the lonely sailors.

Amanda feels no pang of doubt until she reaches the street corner near the barn. Is this adventure a mistake for a still-married woman? Does she just long to hear the music she remembers from so long ago? Or maybe she's there to flirt a bit. That's always part of any dance, isn't it? She feels a level of shame at that desire.

But it's been a while since she's had male companionship. It always gave her a warm feeling. This dance, any dance, is a good place to feel that way again.

This is just good fun, she tells herself as she approaches the building. Just something to do on a Saturday night.

It's also something to do for a woman who's too old, at twenty-three, to travel with the flock of young single girls who stand near the edge of the dance.

It's something to do for a woman who is too young and too much of an outsider to stand with the married female chaperones, talking of families, babies, bank loans, and apple pies. She will be very much alone in the crowd.

Inside the barn, the air is humid. The place wasn't built to hold this many people, and the body heat from the dancers hangs like a fog. Any door or window that can be unlocked and made wider has been propped open to boost airflow. People who aren't dancing stand in doorways, cooling themselves and watching the scene. Most tap their toes or clap.

Amanda makes her way toward a refreshment table. A woman with hair twisted in a steel-gray bun nods a welcome and hands her a glass of punch. Amanda takes it, mostly to have something to do with her nervous hands. She weaves over toward a side wall, where she leans, sips, and watches.

Into the sticky mass, from the other side of the barn, strolls Jeb Thomas, pearl-handled pistol in his boot and fresh photographs tucked into his pocket, courtesy of Devlin Richards and Chen Lu.

Usually a Kodak camera has to be mailed back to the company in Rochester, New York, which then develops the film and mails the photos back along with the camera, freshly loaded with a new roll of film. But Chen Lu did not have the luxury of time. Instead he took the camera to a Boston photographer friend and insisted that he develop the photos that same day. The man protested, saying he only works with glass plates and had no idea what to do with Eastman's newfangled paper-backed film. But with a little experimentation, the photographer was able to develop and print a handful of poor-quality photos.

The photo of the woman with the dark hair is not a good one. But she's recognizable.

Jeb knows she lives somewhere in this part of the city. But the sun is going down now. It's time to wait and relax.

For him, this is both a day off, and a day for union work. Tomorrow he will continue the peculiar and impractical treasure hunt that's been occupying too much of his time. But tonight he pushes it from his mind.

Jeb actually was invited to the dance by a member of a fledgling dockworkers union. He's been offered a chance to speak during the break. Looking around, he realizes that the crowd represents a broad mix of workers, neighborhood people, and even the sons and daughters of ship chandlers and warehouse owners. He knows his usual speech would not be well received in this blended setting and decides to tell the organizers this may not be the best place to make their pitch. He can speak instead at the union's next meeting, to a smaller crew of supportive listeners.

He walks to the edge of the room, leaning back against a rough upright support. The warmth of the place makes him glad he wore a light cotton shirt. He rolls up the white sleeves and glances around the room. Surprisingly the mix is about even, male to female. Union hall dances often end up one-sided, with far too many men milling about uncomfortably and too few women who end up feeling even more uncomfortable and out of their element.

Between songs, Jeb strikes up a conversation with a dockworker. Jeb learns that this particular band, called Bothy

Mountain, has grown popular in recent months. The size of the crowd is partly due to the union's sponsorship, and partly due to the following the band has created, playing in various neighborhoods each weekend.

Jeb scans the crowd and spies several pretty faces. At least two look back at him, eye contact lingering a moment or two. But they're so young. He's thirty now, and it seems all the women near his age are long since married and having their second or third baby. He sees girls dancing that can't be any older than fifteen or sixteen. He shakes his head.

Times like these, the reality of his life on the road hits home. Never having a solid relationship. Never settling down. And now too old, he knows, to be chasing some flaxen-haired teenager.

His eyes linger on one dancing girl with flowing auburn hair, twirling so fast her skirt creates a perfect bell shape around her legs. She is a moment of timeless beauty.

But so innocent too.

Jeb's way of living, meager and nomadic as is, has given him a worldliness that few people ever experience. He feels a certain smug satisfaction in that, in spite of the loneliness. It gives him a confidence, and a certain stride in his step, which people notice.

Amanda decides to get a second glass of punch. The fiddle music seems to grow louder as she walks toward the table. Elsewhere in the city, at places like the Boston Music Hall, the instrument would be called a violin. It would be held properly under the chin, set loosely on the shoulder.

But in this barn it's a fiddle. Held low. Played more aggressively. Played with more passion, Amanda thinks. The songs are a combination of Irish, Scottish, American traditional, and a sprinkling of ancient sea songs whose lineage is unknown, but which often mention Boston, Dublin, London, or New Orleans.

Refilled glass in hand, she walks through a sudden swirl of dresses. Bell shapes appear and disappear as the music changes. Men twirl women roughly, the same way they wind the winches on their ships.

The smell grows sweaty and earthy. The pounding beat makes the wooden floor bounce as a hundred feet thump down in unison. Amanda moves along the edge of the dance, nearly pushed to the wall by all the people. Her nervousness dissipates. No one is looking at her. No one judges her or her singleness. She is but one more face in the crowd, in a place where all types of people have gathered. It's the difference between a city and a small town.

She relaxes, sips her punch, and chats, as best she can, with other people. Eventually she sees a face she recognizes. It's Martha Stokes, daughter of the man who accompanied her to the antique store. She walks over and greets Martha warmly.

Across the room, Jeb Thomas scans the women and looks for ones that are closer to his own age. There aren't many, but he does see a few fine, hearty women—women he'd dance with in a moment, given half a chance. He tries to see who is wearing wedding rings, but hands move too fast.

Best to proceed cautiously.

He narrows his prospects down to about three women. One is stout, with a very pretty face. The others are thinner and just a bit younger than he.

There's also a woman with dark hair near the corner. He watches her for a while and finds himself fascinated. The hair. The gestures. The smile. The laughter he can't quite hear. He sees both a shyness and a confident demeanor, and it seems to charge the air around her.

He stares, enthralled, for over three minutes before something occurs to him. He pulls the brownish photos from his pocket and shuffles through them, finding the one of the girl. He looks down, then up at her, then back down again. It must be her. It would make sense since she lives near here. He can't be sure—the photo is blurred and taken from the side. But the resemblance is uncanny. He slides the photos back into his pocket and heads in that general direction, toward the corner, by way of the refreshment table.

Chapter 27

The Dance

The music is hypnotic to Amanda. The noise makes it difficult to talk with Martha, so they stop, turning to watch the fiddle player as he starts a solo. Then the voice of the singer merges back in, a deep tenor, resonating off the walls as he sings of ships and waves and wasted lives. There is a straightforward cadence to the music, and the dancers keep time with it.

Two lines start to form along the length of the hall. It's not square-dancing exactly. It's a line dance. A contra dance with men and women facing "contrary" to one another.

The contra dance of each community is slightly different. It's different from town to town and different from sailors to farmers. A line dance carries with it a nuance that reflects the mores and customs of the local folk.

She senses something different here. Something unique. This community is transient. These are people who barely know each other, and who hope to change that by the end of the evening.

Someone grabs her hand, pulling Amanda into the line of women. More than one man attempts to line up directly across from her. The lines move inward, and she smiles as a tall man with a beard reaches out to her. She grasps both his outstretched hands. Everyone along the line does the same with their opposing partner. It forms a long cathedral ceiling of arms. She's not sure what to do exactly, but feels game for the adventure. She lets the tall man lead, his large hands holding hers tightly. In time to the music, they sidestep up the length of the line, then twirl and fall back, edging down the line again, still clapping. There are more men than women in the facing rows, so the next time she's paired with a different man as they skip up the middle again.

The banjo player breaks into a long solo with the crowd stopping to clap. The lines grow with more and more people, spilling out the door and into the lawn. As the solo ends, the line dance starts again with a roar. She can't tell who she's across from anymore. She reaches out and makes the run with whoever grabs her hands—a different man each time. Sidestepping, twirling, repeating, and laughing out loud.

She grows bolder. With each new face, she makes eye contact. Smiling.

Men.

Good lord, she remembers men. She remembers what they feel like and smell like up close. A silly thing to think, but it's true. She likes holding their hands and smiling at them. She likes the closeness. The rough feeling of their faces. She likes their strength, even when it seems dangerous.

Since her marriage, her ability to flirt has grown rusty. She's avoided such eye contract, preferring the comfort and assurance of a wifely existence. Now she's practicing her wiles again. Pressed back into it, she starts to enjoy it. Each new face holds an opportunity. Each of those faces must have a name. She can learn those names if she wishes. Or she can move down the line, reaching for the next hand and a new prospect.

She feels seventeen again. She's in an orchard, and there is ripe fruit everywhere. Lonely sailors and fishermen, many earnest and hardworking, are looking for someone just like her. They seek an excuse to come ashore and stay there for good.

A new song starts. The contra dance continues.

Eventually she ends up across from a nice-looking man with clean work clothes. He seems to have purposely maneuvered through the crowd to end up across from her. She likes the way he looks—a man who keeps up appearances and who bothers to make sure his shirt and hands are clean. That's too rare. She smiles as they clasp hands and make the run up the line. For this one, she does indeed wonder about his name. She wonders what kind of fruit grows on this particular tree.

As the line comes around again, she can see that they will be paired up once more. He obviously has switched positions in the line to make this happen, and she laughs. As they sidestep through the barn and onto the lawn, she tells him he's a troublemaker, and he nods in agreement.

The fiddler finally slows, arm tired from his long performance. The dancers slowly break off into pairs and small groups, and the band takes a break. The man she's been dancing with motions toward the nearly empty punch bowl, and Amanda suddenly realizes how thirsty she is and nods yes. She also notices the broadness of the man's shoulders as they walk toward the table.

Amanda feels dizzier than she should be. Is it the summer heat? Or has someone poured a little whiskey into the punch bowl?

Oh, so what if they have.

"I don't think they expected this many people," the man says, handing her a glass cup with a curly handle.

"No," she says. "I certainly wasn't expecting this kind of crowd when I heard the music. The Fourth of July does bring people out."

They look out over the scene, or pretend to. Gazes trail back toward each other, and they both laugh.

"So you just heard the music and decided to come? You didn't know about the dance?"

"No. I didn't even know this barn was here. I haven't been in the neighborhood long." She notices him looking at her hand. She wonders if there's any indentation or tan line that might betray that a ring used to reside there. She looks at his hand too and sees nothing but eligibility. It's a silly ritual, but it's the first checkpoint on a long list of steps one takes when learning to dance anew.

They make small talk about the weather and the neighborhood and then stroll toward the door. Much of the crowd has spilled out of the barn and onto the grass around the Mariner's House. In the windows of the building, lodgers stand, looking out, watching the crowd take its break beneath the stars.

"So if you aren't from this area, where did you move from?" he asks.

"From the Cape."

"Cape?"

"Cape Cod, silly."

"Yes, yes, of course."

She studies him for a moment. "You aren't from around here either, are you?"

He laughs. "No ... no, I'm not. My dad lived in New England at one time, but I consider myself from the Midwest. Grew up near Chicago mostly. We moved a lot as my dad looked for work."

She nods, swinging her skirt slightly as they walk in a slow circle around the yard.

"That must have been interesting, to travel."

"To him maybe. I didn't like it at the time."

"Did you like your father?" She immediately regrets asking so personal a question.

"Like? Oh … well, I guess so. Yes. He was all right."

"I ask because I barely knew my own father. I mean I did, until I was nine. But he was always away. On ships. And then one day we lost him. I think I did like him. I remember being thrilled whenever he returned. I'd hug him, and he'd always have some trinket for me. But he was nearly a stranger, you know?" She smiles at him in a candid way. "I know that was a silly question to ask. It just popped into my head."

"No, no. Don't think … I mean don't worry about it. It's nice to know what prompted it. And I'm sorry—about your father."

She nods. "It was a long time ago. I'm over it. Just part of my history."

He stops and looks her in the eyes. "Surprised to find you at a dance with mostly sailors. I should think you'd want to stay away from them." He shrugs. "They lead a dangerous life. You'd risk feeling that sort of loss again."

"I guess I didn't know what I was getting into coming into the barn. But I don't think there's any way to avoid risk and possible loss, do you?"

She can see him thinking, deciding what to say next. She finds it entertaining, actually, to feel such attention. She's very glad she decided to come.

"If I may be so bold," Jeb finally says, "you caught my eye because you are different from most of the girls in there. And I do mean girls. It's nice to meet someone your age who isn't living the life of a wife and mother." He sees her stare at the ground suddenly and hopes it wasn't the wrong thing to say. But it's the direction he needs to take the conversation. The next checkpoint in the getting-to-know-you, if there is such a thing. "Not that there's anything ... um ... well ...."

"Look, I ... I was. Okay?" Amanda states honestly. "I was married for almost three years. That's all I can really say right now. Things didn't work out. It happens."

He nods.

"And no, I'm not a mom."

She can see his frown. Even in this dim light, the look is obvious. And all the emotions come rushing in. A separated woman. She shouldn't have said it. But he seemed nice. And she so longed to be honest with him.

Why is a woman in her situation viewed so negatively? Why don't people understand? She isn't trash.

His response surprises her. "I didn't mean to make you feel bad. I actually thought many times growing up that my parents should have separated. I know how it can be. Arguments and tension all the time. It's strange. Society frowns on couples breaking up, but if something doesn't work, then it just doesn't. I know that. You know it too."

Amanda laughs. "That is a very refreshing thing to hear, Mister ...," and she suddenly realizes that she doesn't know this man's name. Here she is dancing with him and talking about things that she rarely mentions to anyone, and she doesn't even know who he is. He shouted a name to her once inside, but it was lost in the music and stomping.

"Thomas," he says. "Jeb Thomas, ma'am. Please to meet you."

He gives a mock bow and she gives a nearly imperceptible curtsey.

"Amanda," she hesitates. "Amanda … Grant." She hasn't used her original last name in a long time. She looks him in the eye. "And I said it's refreshing because I haven't found many men who don't subscribe to society's traditional view. I'm damaged goods, I guess, to most of them. I should be home cooking, cleaning, and having babies."

"And never leaving your home," he laughs.

He stops walking and turns toward her. She doesn't wait for him to continue.

"Don't laugh. That actually *is* what I wanted. I'm not one of those suffragettes who wants women out of the house for good. I was looking forward to living that way once. To being a wife. To running a home …." Her voice trails off.

"So you don't agree with the suffragettes, hmm?"

"I don't know. As a woman, part of me very much likes the idea. I would love to be able to vote. I'd love other job opportunities. But as much as this country has been through in the last thirty years, I'm not sure we could absorb so much social change all at once."

He laughs. "Well, my dear, social change is what I'm all about. Organizing. Union work. Do you know anything about unions?" Jeb looks at her face and thinks of the photo in his pocket. The photo did not do her justice. He knows this must be the same woman, but he almost hopes that it's not. He likes her. He likes talking with her. If things go well, this might be a great opportunity to learn more about the missing box. But if things move too slowly, he might have to complicate the fledgling relationship with theft.

"I know a bit about unions, I guess," she responds, "from the newspapers. Which union are you with?" The very thought of union violence makes her nervous.

"No one group in particular. I'm more of an adviser. A logistics person of sorts who has an understanding of the issues and how unionization works. I point out the injustices that people often don't see. I rally them. I like to think I inspire fairness."

"Is that so?" She fans herself with her open palm. "I imagine that's quite a challenge."

To counter her hint of sarcasm, he drops his voice to a whisper. "You know, in my book, a woman's right to vote is just one more injustice that needs to be corrected."

"Oh really?"

"Yes, really," he smiles. "Wyoming set the standard last year, don't you think? It's just a matter of time and proper organization before it happens here."

"I guess I don't know that much about the whole issue."

He shrugs.

Amanda continues. "I guess I don't know much about what you do either. I don't know how unions form, or why an organizer is needed. I don't know how you might get paid. I sometimes hear people like you labeled as troublemakers. I don't know if that's true, or if it's just talk."

"Oh, it's true, believe me," Jeb says with a wink.

"Yes, Mr. Thomas. I suspected as much," she winks back.

He gives her a crash course in union history. Of factory workers. Of ownership and exploitation—such as he sees it. She nods, with a new swirl of questions rising in her mind.

"How do you make a living doing all of this?" she asks earnestly.

Jeb nods his head. "That's a good question. I guess I don't make much of a living actually. It's more of a calling than anything. Like being a preacher or a soldier. Small unions sometimes pay me to come in and negotiate an alliance with a larger union. Sometimes I talk to the press for them, making sure their message is portrayed in the best light. I carry messages from the larger organizers all across the nation, looking for local chapters. They pay me a bit to do that, though it's usually eaten up by travel costs. Sometimes people ask for me because I've established a bit of a name for myself, though not nearly as big a reputation as Samuel Gompers or Terence Powderly."

He looks at her slyly and says, "You probably make more money than I do."

"Oh, I doubt that. I have no job and no future."

He stops and takes her hand, looking into her eyes. "I don't believe that for a minute. Are you recently separated?"

"Very recently. A matter of days."

"Will you go back to him?"

"No. Not ever."

He looks directly in her eyes in a way that few men seem to know how to do. "Then you just need to see what's suddenly opened up to you. There's much more than you think. More than you even would have found a few years ago."

Much as she enjoys his gaze, to her his words fall like a brick as soon as they leave his mouth.

"Very funny. I don't think much has opened up at all. The prospects for a woman who isn't married by my age are not good."

"Why? How old are you?"

She gazes at him, eyes trying to confirm the brazen rudeness of his question. But she realizes she's the one who brought up the subject of age. "I'm twenty-three, twenty-four in September. Okay?"

"You've got to be kidding. You think you're washed up?"

"Well, maybe. All the girls in my neighborhood were married by nineteen. I was the local spinster at twenty."

"So when you got married at twenty, was it because you wanted to, or because you thought it was the thing to do?"

She gives him a penetrating glance.

"Sorry. None of my business. Forget I asked."

"Goodness, you are a very direct man, aren't you?" She smiles as she sees him look away. "But it's okay. It's a legitimate question, given where I am right now. The answer, I think, is both. I had some very good times with Wayne. That's his name. I wouldn't have married him if I didn't. But yes, I also think I married him because I needed to make a transition. It was time for the next phase of my life, and it was a chance to get out of the slum and out to the country."

Jeb nods, and everything in his demeanor indicates that he understands perfectly. Then he surprises her. "But what if you didn't?"

"What do you mean?"

"You said you needed a transition. That it was time. And that's exactly what society tells you, right? It's what the people around you say all the time, so it makes sense. But was it really the right choice for you? At that time and in that place?"

"I don't know, Mr. Thomas. I thought it was, and I can't second-guess that decision now. Like I said, there were many good months. I don't regret the choice. I only regret the outcome."

They stop near a low wall, and Jeb steps atop the stones. The stance seems quite natural for him as he moves his arms in broad arcs, balancing as they walk again.

"Well, I think it has to change. The world has to change. I think people make bad decisions because of what society pressures them to do. I'm not saying you did, but I see it all the time. I see people giving up farming to work in dark, dangerous factories. I see them give up everything to become slaves to low wages. They relinquish the freedom of what they have, for the uncertainty of industry, which can cast them aside without a warning the second the needs of the business owner change."

She looks up at him. "Standing up there like that … perhaps you could have been a preacher, Mr. Thomas!"

"It happens to people because they feel the pressure," he continues. "In a factory they can work in the winter and maybe stay somewhat warm. They remove the risk of weather. They remove the risk of mortgage payments on a farm. But the workers ignore so many other risks—the risks of being under someone else's control. This risk of not having property of their own, or food that they grow and control. It's all about money, Amanda. Those in control of the money and the factory slowly tighten their grip. The workers slowly lose."

She studies Jeb carefully. "My, you have given this a great deal of thought, haven't you?"

"Well, one doesn't choose a job like mine without thinking long and hard about it. One has to believe in what's right and just."

He hops down from the wall and brazenly takes her arm. She allows it.

"So what brings you to Boston, Mr. Thomas?"

"Union issues, of course. Dockworkers. The usual problems. Long hours with no breaks. Company-owned housing. Owners hiring immigrants at lower wages and displacing the long-timers."

She blinks. "You could be talking another language, for all I know. Yet I remember my father complaining of some of these same issues. I'd hear him in the kitchen late at night, talking to my mother."

"There, you see?"

"In his case, his complaint was against the ship owners. Some would send ships from port to port to port across the ocean or down the coast, without returning home for years at a time. A sailor might think he was leaving for a month only to find plans changing as the voyage stretched on. He might be able to pick up passage home on a different carrier, or he might not. I also remember him complaining about making the sailors help with the unloading, so they wouldn't have to pay dockworkers, even if they had been sailing for days straight. No extra pay for a lot of surprise extra work."

"Exactly. But he couldn't get away from it, could he?"

"No. He kept on sailing, again and again. He talked of quitting, but he had no idea what else he could do."

Jeb picks up her story line like he's heard it and told it many times before. "So your father put up with things—bad things— because no one was speaking for him. No one was looking out for him and helping all the sailors. He put up with it and he traveled more than he wanted and eventually he was lost, and look how that left you."

"What do you mean?"

"I mean things were probably pretty bad for you after he was gone, no? Hard to keep the house. Hard to buy new things. No money coming in, and the company not really looking out for you, save for a few dollars and maybe a turkey at Christmas time."

She looks away. "They … well, they provided some things. Some help."

"Sure, and that too disappeared after a couple years. Maybe a few dollars for a few years. But nothing formal. No one wants to support a widow forever. But your mom and your family—you ended up on your own, didn't you?"

She nods. "We moved to Lowell for a while. My mom worked in the mills. Then we moved back."

"Of course you did. Lowell was set up to provide housing for working single girls. A widow with a family was too hard to accommodate."

He sees her look toward the distance. He knows the look. He's seen it countless times before as he's lectured and prodded and changed the way people think. So he presses on. "So what happened then? Had to move again and again, I'll bet. Maybe had to go live with a relative. You couldn't live in the best part of town. Mom had to take in washing, maybe work in a pub, who knows. Mouths to feed. The neighbors dropping off food and used clothes, to her shame. But she accepted them. For the family. For you. And then what? You, your brothers, and sisters started to trickle away. Before you were ready I'll bet. Dropping out of school. Taking jobs with little training. Getting married. If you have a brother, I'll bet he joined the army. You all grew up too fast because you had to."

"Stop it."

He does, apologizing. He stammers that he didn't mean anything by it. "It's just … just …."

She holds up her hands. "I know, Mr. Thomas. I know. You're passionate. I respect that. And I don't actually disagree with you. But that started hitting a little close to home."

They turn to walk back toward the barn. The music has started again, and the crowd, slightly smaller now, is drifting back inside. Women fan themselves with folded newspapers, and men have their collars wide open and sleeves rolled high.

"Well, anyway, my lady, that's what I do. I guess I get carried away sometimes when I try to explain it. I delve into very personal examples because I know that can help people understand the issues."

"It's fine, really. Don't worry about it."

He slows their walk, not wanting the conversation to end. "I guess what started this was when we talked about what society expects of a woman. Of how you felt you had no options at your young age. That's what we have to change. The options of the working people. The options of women. I want women to have a vote. I want them in my unions. I want them to be able to survive on their own, if they need to, without shame. Or pity. Or gifts from the neighbors. Does that make sense?"

She nods, but only slightly. As they reach the barn door, she turns to him. "Are you tired? Or would you care to dance some more?"

"Tired? Not at all. I could go all night."

With smiles, they step together back into the swirl of bodies, and stay for hours.

Chapter 28

Baby Talk

Swaying.

That's the first thing the stranger senses. A shift, side to side, one side then the other. Like being pushed and pulled. He dreams of being a child in a carriage, pushed along by his mother. He tries to see and understand the world around him. In the stranger's dream the day is sunny and safe. He is incapable of speech, so he just laughs and coos. He places his hands on all the people or things he can reach. He likes the smiles he receives when he does this. He likes touching this world and exploring it. That's all he understands for now. Being a child. Touching. Learning. Slowly understanding.

As the dream child, he continues handling the things he can reach and gathering smiles from passing strangers. It's a rewarding game. But suddenly someone doesn't smile back. Suddenly someone hisses and yells at his touch. Then everything dissolves. What did he do wrong?

The illusion changes. He's older now, and dreams of riding a borrowed bicycle, flying down a hill and laughing. Feet off the pedals. Wind in his hair. The hill seems to go on forever. There is a sensation of other children rushing along somewhere beside him. Laughter in his ears. Smell of apple blossoms in the air. He outraces them all and shouts out his victory. But the words come out all jumbled. His voice is jumbled. His tongue seems fat and out of place. Then the bottom of the hill looms, and he doesn't know how to stop. He shouldn't have done this. He shouldn't have borrowed the bike and gone so fast. He feels himself crashing, crashing and falling. Then there is pain, and back to darkness.

The swaying motion returns. He becomes aware of it, ignores it. Then comes back to it again. He can't understand this. Is he lost? Is he safe? Is he floating? At least he feels warm. The whole world seems soft. He's content to dream a little longer. He dreams of many things, ill-defined things, but always with a combination of warmth and happiness, suddenly interrupted by danger.

Always a new danger.

Slowly, the stranger begins to suspect that he's half-awake. It's like no consciousness he's felt before. He doesn't know where he is. Or what he is. He's not even sure who he is. He is a floating speck, with some level of jumbled consciousness.

The bed is wet. His jaw is sore, like it's been clenched for hours.

Wait. A bed? He's in a bed? Is that right? Yes. That's it.

Awake. That's what he wants now. To be awake. This in-between thing, not awake and not fully asleep, is maddening. It's calm here, but he needs to escape the comfort of these dreams just long enough to know.

Know what? He isn't sure. But he needs to know … something. He has to awaken. He simply has to.

His eyes are heavy, and they refuse to stay open. But before they close … wood. Yes, that's what he saw. He manages to open them once, then twice. So heavy.

Yes, it's wood alright. He knows about wood, somehow, and this wood sits maybe eighteen inches from his face. Ugly wood. Rough. Heavy. Black goo between the boards.

He sleeps again, and dreams of snow. Soothing coolness. He needs that. Snow blankets the world. It erases everything.

Hours.

185

Has it been hours? He awakens again. It seems later. It can't be earlier, can it? Which way does time run anyway? The concept of time is difficult. Understanding anything is difficult.

But he does know what wood is.

How does he know it?

He thinks he understands distance too. That's how he knew how close he was to the wood. He knows how to measure distance. Yes. There's the wood again. Eighteen inches, definitely. So he *is* capable of understanding some things. A few things maybe. And it's ugly wood. Right? A rough beam. And what is that goo? Some kind of pitch? He knows that word too. He sees six boards with the gooey pitch in between.

The dream state tries to erode. The mind tries to recall.

He thinks about what he knows so far. He understands distance, and maybe materials for some reason—wood and pitch—and now … how to add numbers.

Why the hell can't he wake up?

He feels cold. Why is the bed wet?

He hears voices. He doesn't understand them. Maybe he really is still a baby, and language remains difficult. He uses his hands and tries to reach out and touch his world again. But it's too tiring. Maybe later.

But as sleep comes again, something registers. It's not baby talk he hears.

French. It's French. He seems to remember enough to know that. Maybe that's why he doesn't understand the words. He's not a baby, and they're not talking baby talk. They must be saying words in French that he doesn't understand.

In his new dream, he is not a child anymore. He is a man. Tall, strong. He stands in a field. He starts walking, walking faster, and then running. He speeds from one knoll to the next through ankle-high grass. Is it new wheat? Is it a field left to seed?

He looks out from each small knoll as he reaches its crest, but he can't find a house. Or a road. Or anything. There's just more field. And more, and more. Running with no plan. He finally grows tired and sinks to his knees. It's lonely here. No one at all but him. Nothing. The dream didn't end in danger this time, but he is, instead, quite alone. Perhaps the French speakers will come back and try to talk with him.

The next time he opens his eyes to look at the wood, the voices are closer. They are in the room with him. Suddenly just realizing that he is in a room and that the place is even called a room makes him happy. This is progress, he thinks. He's moving more toward awake than toward sleep.

He turns and sees a man in blue pants talking to a man wearing white pants. That's all he can see for now, just the pants. He lacks the energy to lift his gaze higher.

"*Tu penses qu'il va mouri ?*" one of the pairs of pants says.

"*J'y ai cru pendant dix jours, mais il persiste encore,*" replies the other.

The words make his mind race. He thinks back … way back. To school. Long ago. Lessons. A teacher. He remembers lessons of some sort that might help him make sense of these words, if he could just remember them. One of the words starts to sink in. They speak of dying, these men in the room. Who they are talking about, he does not know.

"*Comment peut-il vivre s'il ne mange pas?*"

"Le cuisinier lui versa de la soupe. Hmm... Peut-être que ça suffit."

He tries to raise his head to look at them. The men notice this and look at each other.

"Can you see me?" one of them says, his words heavily accented but understandable. He speaks English.

The stranger on the bed nods, hair falls over his face, greasy and clumped.

The one in the blue pants wears a blue coat as well. He is tall. He squats down beside the bed to look at him. The stranger on the bed reaches out to touch him. The blue pants man does not hiss or growl in response. Instead he takes hold of the hand.

This is good, the stranger thinks. Touching. Learning.

The swaying continues. The tall Frenchman grabs the bed to steady himself. And this simple action explains so much to the stranger.

It isn't just me, he thinks from the bed. The whole room is swaying back and forth. We're rocking. Back and forth. Up and down too.

"What is your name?" blue pants asks.

The man in the bed thinks about this for a bit. Names. What are names? What are they used for? He knows the answer to this. At least he thinks he does. But thinking is so hard right now. Just looking around and reaching out to touch has exhausted him. He needs to put all this thinking away for a while. He needs to leave this and go back to the dreams. Maybe he can visit again.

He closes his eyes, and drifts away.

He feels a patting, patting, patting on his face. He doesn't want to awaken. This feeling of patting is annoying. It's getting in the way of the new dreams that he wants to slide into to enjoy.

The patting becomes slapping. There's shouting. He doesn't want to awake, but the slapping keeps demanding something of him. The slapping calls him back and forces him awake, and he hates the feeling. It makes him react. *Open your eyes* it seems to say, and he finally does …. "Damn it! Who? What? What?"

The stranger stuns himself. He spoke! He heard it himself. This means that he is capable of speech, and that he speaks English. This changes things remarkably. He does need to learn more. The child of his deep dreams needs to go away for a while. The stranger knows now that he needs to wake up, finally, and to speak again. His tired eyes open. The other men stare at him in disbelief.

"Where am I?" the stranger asks.

"You are on zee clipper ship *Fleur de Montagne*. It is seven in the evening."

He understands all of this. Maybe it was spoken in his language? Or maybe he can suddenly speak French? He isn't sure which.

"Why?" he continues.

"Do you remember? Anything?"

It's so hard for the stranger to understand this man in the blue coat. His voice so low. His accent so heavy.

"No."

"Nothing?"

"My arms are bruised. I remember being lifted. Pulled …."

"Yes. Into a dory."

"I don't understand."

"You have had a terrible fever. You have been unconscious for many days. We thought you would die. You still may. Your lungs are heavy with infection."

In spite of the dire predicament, the stranger seems happy with this answer. It explains many things to him. The wood he saw. The rocking. He knows now that he is in a berth on a boat. He has a fever, so that explains why he can barely think. That's all he needs to know for now. End of the conversation. So tired.

He closes his eyes, but the patting returns. Why won't this Frenchmen leave him alone?

"Try to wake up. Monsieur! It will be good for your mind to be awake for a bit. Do you remember anything else? What happened to you?"

"I …." He thinks. He does remember, sort of. Tiny bits and pieces come back. "I remember a gun."

"Someone shooting at you?"

"No … no. I was doing the shooting, I think. A shotgun. Two shots. In the boat."

He closes his eyes. The two Frenchmen look at each other. The tall man leans closer to the other.

"I'm not sure what we have here," he says in his low French whisper, "but we may want to contact an inspector when we make port. Perhaps there was foul play involved. This American may be innocent, or he may be a criminal. The inspector can decide."

The man in the bed, sweating again, hears this and understands it. Does this mean he does indeed speak French? Or did the tall man just continue his conversation in English? No … they said American, and this too makes sense. When he wakes up, he will speak whatever language an American is supposed to speak. Or maybe he won't speak at all, ever again. It doesn't matter. Nothing matters but sleep.

Chapter 29

Family History

The next level of the box opens quite suddenly.

Amanda isn't sure exactly how it happened. She was sort of holding it upside down and maybe twisting it a bit. The second drawer simply popped open and a wad of papers fluttered down to her quilt.

It's about one in the afternoon on July 5th. She had a very late start that morning. The hours of dancing took their toll, and she slept in a bit. Sleeping in for her means 9:00 a.m. rather than seven. By nine thirty she was out walking the streets, visiting shop after shop to look for work. She didn't come home with a job, but she did find a few prospects. One of the shop owners even asked her to stop back in three days.

Amanda grabs up the fallen papers from her bed and turns them over. The handwriting is crisp and neat. There is a title at the top that simply reads "Legacy." She glances over the first few sentences, and they seem to indicate that this is a story. Unlike the diary, it's a longer narrative.

Besides the main handwriting, there's something penciled along the top margin. Amanda walks to the window to see if she can read it. The text is faded, and she has to step onto the roof and into the direct sunlight. It's a scrawled note—an afterthought of sorts—that attempts to introduce the document. She starts to read.

Dear Elizabeth,

You, dear sister, always told me that I should be a writer. I don't think your request was related to any particular talent that I possess. I think you simply had a romantic notion about writers and thought we should have one in the family. To date, this is the only attempt I've made at writing—at least for anything other than a technical document. Now that I've tried it, I have to say that I find the whole writing process confusing and too much of a struggle. It may appeal to some people, but I don't think it's for me. I will always prefer numbers and experiments.

Write about what you know, you said. So this attempt at a story, rough as it is, is roughly pieced together from the many things I've heard over the years. Our father once told me about what he learned of my birth. Our mother often described Father's drinking and the error of his ways. This story is an assemblage of many of those tales. It's how I picture a special day in my mind. It's probably all wrong, but it's the only story of the event that I have. Do tell me if it looks familiar to you!

Sorry to disappoint on the writing front, but I do have my journal, which I continue to keep. If I'm not able to mail this story to you soon, perhaps I will just give it to you the next time I see you, and we can both have a good laugh.

- V.M.

Intrigued, Amanda unfolds the pages and the story, and starts to read.

————

Legacy

Victor Marius joined the party sometime in the spring of 1865. At least that's the way his father, Eli, likes to tell the story.

"Joined the party."

Life is a rich, varied, and booze-fueled party to the elder Marius. Work, in contrast, is something he tolerated.

As far as Eli is concerned, people aren't so much born as thrust through a door into lives they never chose. Rather than fight the lottery called life, he believes people should relax and enjoy their situations, be they rich or of meager means. Life isn't something to be improved upon or fretted about. It's something to be gripped with both hands and experienced.

Eli was twenty-six years old the day he heard about his son's birth. He sat beside the warmth of a late-night fire as it sputtered and sparked in a metal pail. That pail sat on the deck of a troop ship that had no name. The ship was docked in Annapolis harbor in the waning days of the War of the Rebellion, and he was a lowly deckhand. Worse, he was a sailor with nothing much to do. The troops were in the field. Lee was nearly defeated, and Eli, along with a handful of others, was left watching the ship and waiting for ... well, they weren't quite sure. They were just waiting.

The letter, with news from home, was welcome when it arrived. Eli had not heard from his wife, Hannah, for several months. He'd come to believe that he never would. Life never had been much of a party to Hannah. Eli's hardworking, sensible wife had grown tired of his festive, unfocused ways. She could never share his devil-may-care outlook on life, nor his taste for wine.

On the troop ship, Eli was always one of the last ones to turn in. Even if someone else had the late watch, he and a few other night owls would stoke the coals in the tiny deck bucket, play a little fiddle music, and talk. There was not much else to worry about since the boys over in Petersburg finally had the Rebels on the run. The sailors remaining in Annapolis with the troop ships were protecting a harbor they knew would never be invaded. Many of the men complained. They wanted to be closer to the action. Eli didn't understand that. Here they were, getting paid, with all the vittles they wanted and a place to sleep. There were no real threats to deal with, and there were dozens of men, all about the same age, just looking to do their minimal duties and to have a good ole time. To hell with the frontlines, Eli thought. He was quite happy right here.

That's why Eli was still awake, laughing and singing, when a supply boat returned from Baltimore. It held fresh meat, a pile of turnips, five crates of rifles, and—best of all—a bundle of month-old letters. News from the North. The men who were still awake jumped up and pawed through the mail like starving animals.

"I'm a father!" Eli shouted to his mates after ripping open an envelope with his wife's handwriting. Somewhere in his youth, he'd at least learned to read. He only made it to the third grade, but his mother had often read to him by lamplight, and she had helped him learn the words. Sometimes he'd even read the mail of other sailors aloud to them if they couldn't do it themselves.

"Look at this," he said, spinning around and shaking the letter in the air. "I got me a new baby boy. A goddamned son, can you believe it?" There were backslaps and whoops all around. Someone found a cigar, which was thrust, already lit, into Eli's mouth as he continued to spin in a circle, arms up and yelling toward the sky.

"A god-damn boy! I'm a father, men! I'm a daddy!"

After a bottle of rye made a few rounds and the late best wishes were delivered, Eli found a quiet spot to sit down to read the full letter. As he held it, he still silently wondered if he'd ever see his wife again. She'd gone north several months earlier—way north from their Pennsylvania home. She was tired of waiting for his return, she said, and not entirely sure if she wanted to pick up where they'd left off since he was never around anyway.

She also doubted that he was responsible enough to raise a family. Her words hurt, even though he'd long harbored the very same doubts about himself. He stared into space for a moment and then started reading the letter again from the beginning. It was not exactly one of those letters—the breakup kind all soldiers dread. But it seemed to be heading in that direction.

Boston, he thought. So that's where she went, to live with that damn spinster aunt of hers. What the hell?

He realized, after reading a bit, that it probably was the aunt who had written the letter. Hannah had only addressed the envelope and seemed to have dictated the text, which was in different handwriting. The aunt had always been well aware of their marital problems and had been very supportive of her niece. Eli sensed a certain nastiness in the words that Hannah would have been too proper to actually mark on paper.

At the end of the letter, the words abruptly changed. It seemed they were no longer coming from Hannah's lips. The color of the ink changed slightly, and the old shrew aunt went into great detail about the delivery. She told how Hannah wasn't able to stay awake through the pain of a torn cervix, nor was she able to stay lucid through the infection and fever that followed. The aunt's words seemed to blame him for all of this.

He bit his lip and read on. The attending doctor was generous with the morphine after the injuries. An exhausted, shivering Hannah slept soundly for five days after Victor's debut.

A hastily hired wet nurse managed to keep the baby alive, even taking him home with her for nearly two weeks. When he read those words, Eli slowly realized how close he had come to losing Hannah. And he realized, with guilt, how much he loved her, and how foolish she was for loving the likes of him.

Eli wouldn't learn until much later that, in all the worry and confusion, Victor's exact birth date had never been recorded. The weeks blended together. The family's preoccupation with Hannah's health erased the vague recollections of the birth itself. Victor was a spring baby. Months later, that's all anyone really remembered. Victor Marius joined the party sometime in the spring of that year.

Eli sighed and threw the letter in the fire, but he tucked the envelope into his cap, somehow feeling closer to Hannah by keeping her handwriting nearby.

"A Goddamn boy," Eli muttered to himself as he placed another broken board on the fire. "A son." He tried to settle down for a nap on the deck, under the stars on that warm Maryland night, but there was so much to think about. So many decisions to make. Would he go back to her? Should he?

"How 'bout that? Name's Victor, huh? Yeah, that's a good name, I reckon. A winner. Hope he lives up to it." The new father laughed out loud. "Victor. Ha! Beats the hell out of Eli, don't it?"

He shivered, then again pulled his nearly empty bottle out from under the blanket and lifted it toward the sky. "Well, here's to ya, Victor. Welcome to the party, son. Hope to see you some day. After the war. After everything. Damn world really is changing fast, boy. Hope you can keep up with it. I sure as hell can't."

Amanda slowly refolds the note. She smiles slightly as she places it back in the box, which she then studies, trying to figure out how she actually opened the latest level.

So now she has new information to absorb about this mysterious Mr. Marius. Like her, he grew up in Boston. She now knows his father's name. She now knows that he had a sister. His dad was a veteran of the bloody War Between the States. Nothing unusual about that part of the story. Every man of a certain age seemed to be a veteran of the conflict.

Eli Marius. Father of Victor. She wonders if he's still alive. She wonders if Victor's sister Elizabeth is still alive. She wishes she had time to look them up. Maybe she could return his belongings to them. But for now, she must focus on finding work and a new place to live.

Chapter 30

Awake

The small-town doctor and the French police inspector arrive at the harbor at France's Port de Brest at about the same time. They nod to each other, the doctor slowing his carriage as the inspector urges his own horse up alongside. They both tie off to a low rail and speak in the low tones of official greeting. Then they walk toward a dock where a small tender awaits. Two sailors sit, oars at the ready, prepared to row back to their ship.

The *Fleur de Montagne* is anchored about 200 meters out in the harbor. An overzealous harbormaster prohibited the ship from approaching the pier, fearing that the sick man on board might be contagious. The captain has assured the local officials that the man is simply ill because he spent two terrible days in the water, and that seawater and exhaustion took their toll on his lungs, infecting them. The harbormaster says he will wait for the doctor's report before making his decision.

The delay complicates departure for everyone aboard, and the sailors of the ship seem ready to toss the sick man overboard.

The ride out to the ship is quiet. Neither the doctor nor the police inspector speaks. They know each other from the often sordid tasks of public health and safety. They often do not agree on many things, yet both complete their tasks with grim determination. As they near the ship, they study the faces of the men who gather along the starboard rail. What they see is annoyance and anger, not an epidemic.

On board, the captain puts on a friendly face and greets them. The doctor receives assurances that the man was a victim of circumstance, not disease.

"Yes, yes. I understand," the doctor says. "But of course," he looks at the police inspector, "I have to withhold judgment until I actually examine him."

"Step this way."

The captain tells the inspector of the circumstances that have prompted his involvement. The stranger mentioned a gun. He was found adrift with no real story to tell. The doctor will judge his health while the police will judge the logic of any tale he may try to tell.

Below, the stranger they are there to meet is seated on the edge of his bunk, arms on his knees and head in his hands. He looks pale and gaunt.

The doctor speaks first. The tall, blue-pants sailor acts as interpreter while other men crowd in behind them.

"Are you feeling better?" he asks, pulling a small stool up to the edge of the bunk.

The patient looks confused when he has to wait for every question to be filtered through the interpreter. But it gives him a little extra time to think. He nods. "A bit better, yes. I tried walking just now. I was able to for a bit, but then had to sit down."

The doctor rummages through his bag and takes out a stethoscope. He listens to lungs and heart, stoic face showing neither compassion nor pity.

"Do you have a name?"

"I think so," he says. "I mean ... I know I must. But I'm having trouble recalling everything. I feel like I'm drunk and ready to pass out and I can't shake the feeling.

The doctor looks in the man's mouth, motioning for a lamp to be brought closer.

"So do you care to share this information with us?"

The patient waits for the tongue depressor to be removed, then asks, "Can you tell me why the policeman is here?"

The doctor looks in the stranger's nose and ears too and then feels around his neck. With a gruff snort, he stands. "He'll live, and he has nothing communicable. After all your other business here is completed, I request that this man be brought to my office for treatments of heliotherapy and cod liver oil."

The doctor then looks the man in the eye. "You're lucky to be alive, sir, but it does look to me like your fever is nearly broken. That's a good sign."

With that, the police inspector steps forward. He sits on the same stool and studies the man carefully. The staring goes on so long and so silently that the man finally looks away, then looks back again. He makes eye contact in a defiant stare-down.

"So why won't you tell us your name?" the inspector asks.

"I didn't say that I wouldn't. I'm still remembering things. And I also want to know why you want to talk with me."

The inspector nods slowly. "Merely a formality, I assure you. The circumstances of your rescue and some nagging recollections that you shared during your recovery are enough to prompt ... let's say ... some questions—that's all. You have not been charged with anything. I imagine you won't be charged at all if you cooperate."

"I'm ready to. Just ask me your questions. I hope I'm able to answer them."

The inspector nods. "Let's start with a simple one. Why were you in the ocean, so far from land?"

"My ship sank."

Troubling glances are exchanged all around.

"When and where?"

"June 17, two days out of Massachusetts, near Georges Bank. We went down in a pounding squall."

The inspector tugs at his chin. "Longer ago than we thought. That certainly must have been terrifying."

The man nods. "You have no idea. Like being in cold, dark quicksand."

"Did it go down quickly?"

"No. We fought the intruding water for a long time. And even when we lost, it didn't head straight for the bottom. That helped me."

"How so?"

"I wasn't on deck. I was …." The man squints, trying to remember. He still feels quite dizzy, and this is the longest period of conscious thought he's had for days and days. "The memory is too vague. It's like my thoughts are coated in slippery grease. They just slide away before I can gasp them."

"You said you were near Georges Bank. What if I told you that you were found far from there? Maybe 200 miles?"

He looks back at the inspector blankly. "I don't know. So what if you did tell me that?"

The inspector raises an eyebrow. "I should think it would make your story harder to believe, sir. Unlikely you would have drifted that far."

The stranger considers this. "Unlikely, but not unheard of, given the winds and waves of that storm."

"What was the name of the ship?"

"It was …," his voice trails off. His head hurts. He can picture the ship. Solid but rusty here and there. He pictures the gold name plate on the ship. But the name escapes him. Instead, he sees the face of the engineer in the boiler room. The deckhands too. The cook. He sees a butterfly for some reason, and a dead seagull.

"I … I guess I don't remember."

"Don't remember?" The inspector leans close. "Surely a man who remembers sinking in the middle of the ocean would remember a bit more about how he got there. Why, I'd think it would be one of the defining moments in a man's life. No? Yet you don't remember the name of the ship? You don't remember where you were on board? Where you were going? How you got off the ship?"

"It will come to me. Maybe there are newspaper accounts that you could check."

The inspector decides to change the subject. "Tell me about the gun."

"The what?"

"The gun. You shot someone, no?"

"No!"

"Then someone shot at you? Maybe you leapt overboard to escape?"

The patient thinks about this. No. He has no memory of that. No memory at all of a g—

"Wait … a gun … yes."

"You apparently mentioned a gun to these men. The sea can make a man do funny things. It's been known to make men go mad. More than once I've heard of men who killed everyone on their ship, then dove overboard in despair. That wouldn't be your story, would it, my good man? Your destiny of sorts?"

The man shakes his head in denial after hearing the translation. "No sir. Not at all. And I resent your implication that I might be that sort of man."

The inspector stands. He places a hand on the overhead beam and leans over his detainee. His voice grows louder.

"Then tell me, sir, what sort of man are you? And what became of are your shipmates?"

The stranger stares into the distance. "Drowned." His head hurts, and it falls down into his hands.

"Enough of this," the doctor interrupts. "He needs treatment."

"He'll get it! I just want to know about the damn gun!"

"It was a shotgun. All right?"

All eyes turn toward the patient as he speaks. He lifts his head again and looks eye to eye at the inspector. It's an earnest look. He is a man who is slowly waking up, and slowly starting to remember.

"It was a short, double-barrel percussive shotgun. Just cock and pull. I used it in panic."

The inspector sits back down and listens.

"I do remember that much," the stranger says. His enthusiasm hints at a real memory that is slowly coming to light. "I was stuck deep inside the ship. Right near my bunk. The ceiling had folded down. The water was coming in, and it just wouldn't stop." His eyes change a bit. They became unfocused. The memory is obviously painful. If the others in the room didn't believe his story at first, they start to now. Either that, or this man is a talented liar.

"I ... I couldn't get out. Water coming in through the doorway, pressing in like a cold, giant hand. It kept shoving me back and back. That water outweighed me. It outlasted me."

He gestures with wide arcs. "Behind me was a porthole, not much larger than the top of a spittoon. There was no way out of there. I know—I tried and tried. I could barely get my head to pass through. The water came in there too. I was just stuck, stuck in that compartment like a damn rat." He shivers.

"How long did this go on?"

"I don't know. I just waited. The water came in, and I waited. Filled up the room, until I was floating with my mouth up toward the ceiling, just trying to suck in what little air I could find." He thinks about this for a moment. "Well, I suppose it was 'up' in some sense, but it wasn't really near the ceiling where I was finding the air. The ship was listing, listing something awful to the port side. So the air space was trapped near a corner of the ceiling and the top of one wall. It was just a tiny pocket, and I had my face pressed right into it."

He looks around the room, face to face. Looking for some sign that they believe him. What he sees instead is personal fear. The sailors in the room have all had nightmares just like the one he lived. They listen in pity and trepidation. The tall sailor continues translating furiously, gesturing with his hands when the words didn't quite fit.

205

"So then that damned ship, she started going down, you know? Just settled over completely on her side, and kept settling, farther down into the water like it was denting into a gray pillow. Your mind won't accept what it sees because you never think it can happen to you. Then it got darker. Light from the porthole, what little there was, just sort of got swallowed up by the water. I knew we were under. I was there for a long time, sucking up the air from that little corner of the cabin until it turned stale. Maybe fifteen minutes, maybe more. I don't know. I felt waves of panic come, followed by waves of peace. Then the cycle repeated. It's strange. You eventually accept what's happened, but you don't die yet, and then the reality of what you've accepted settles in, and you start to panic once again. A man's much better off dying fast than going slowly like that. Too much time to think."

He sees the other sailors nod.

"So it was gray and cold and I finally looked around. All around—I don't know why. Maybe just to see the last of it. To say good-bye. I tried to swim up the companionway one last time, but it was too far, and the ceiling was crushed too low. I kept turning back, lungs on fire by the time I returned to the stale air pocket again. I cursed the room because it wouldn't let me go.

"Then the sinking stopped. At least, I think it did. We just sort of hung there, maybe forty feet down. I don't know how long. I was light-headed. Just waiting for the dreaded drowning to start.

"I tried the porthole again. Willing myself to squeeze through it. I tried a shoulder first that time and then tried to squeeze my head behind it. Nothing worked. No room. Just as I let myself drift back toward the last of the stale air, I saw it in the dim, dim light. Right there, mounted on the wall—the shotgun. It belonged to one of the sailors who liked to fish. I grabbed it, not even sure what I was going to do with it, but I had a vague idea that I could maybe do something.

"With the ship on its side, the porthole was just a few inches above me. The room kept shifting, and the last of my air pocket had slid across the wall from the corner and was starting to bubble out the hole. I kicked hard to force the gun above my head and into the disappearing air. I didn't know if it would fire after being underwater, and if it did, I didn't know if the heavy birdshot would just ricochet off the metal sides, tearing me to shreds. But I didn't care."

The man stops talking for a moment and looks around at the faces of the sailors. He starts talking directly to them, not to the doctor or policeman. They are the ones who most understand what he was about to say. He speaks earnestly, hesitating every sentence or two, for the translation to catch up.

"Believe me ... I thought about using that gun a different way. I thought of turning it on myself, ending it all, avoiding the suffering that I knew was coming as that air ran out. I almost did that, and I don't think anyone here would blame me if I had. Would you?"

The translator mimed a gun at his temple. A few of the sailors' heads nodded. They understood.

"But I had to know. I had to know if I could blast through that metal. I had to at least try. I couldn't make a new hole that was large enough. But maybe I could enlarge that porthole that was already there. My foot was against the top of a bunk as I took aim with the first barrel, holding the gun up into the three inches of airspace above me. I aimed at the right side, at about three o'clock. When the gun fired, the noise in that small space was deafening. But the plan worked. It blasted a hand-sized hole in the side, punching out a chunk of the bronze frame around the port in the process. I did the same on the other side, this time aiming at about nine o'clock. Besides the two holes, I was able to tear away the rest of the bronze ring, which gave me another little bit of space. I let the gun sink and reached down to touch the opening. It was jagged, but it was there. Head *and* shoulders might fit now. The metal tore at me hard as I tried to wiggle though. It seemed to take forever and half my shirt was torn off, scraping the hell out of my skin. I saw slight light above and dizzily swam toward the surface."

He looks from face to face, then points at the ocean outside the window. "I tell you, even if you had a full breath of air, coming up forty feet to the surface is quite a trial. But I didn't have anything close to a full breath. Coming up when you've been breathing stale air, and when you wasted time trying to climb out, that there is a true nightmare. My whole body was screaming at me. I felt like I had been sealed in rubber. I kicked and stroked, and all my brain wanted to do was scream at me to breathe. It insisted that I breathe, even if it was to just breathe water. That was another chance I had to end it, right there. Just inhale the water and be at peace. Who knows what it is that keeps a man going?

"But the surface finally came. And the gasp of fresh air tasted sweet even as it hurt my lungs. I can't describe the feeling. It was like sugar had been sprinkled in the wind. I could taste more sweetness with every breath. It was good, and I had escaped. The waves rose and the rain pounded in my face. I felt blood on my arms and shoulders and pain in the cuts on my back. But I didn't care.

"The wind pushed at me and I just let it push. I was free again. I was alive."

"What did you do then?" the translator asked, practically ignoring the police inspector.

"I just floated. All night. Found a board eventually, and then another. I clung to them. I never saw another soul from the ship. I

208

have no idea if any of the others survived. I truly hope some did. I know some days passed. I remember the sunrises and sunsets, then the lack of water. I remember accidental mouthfuls of salty sea. It all took its toll. If it hadn't been for your ship finding me, all would have been lost."

"So what was the ship's name? Do you remember now?"

"Yes. I do remember. It was called the *Gossamer*."

"Surely you could check this story out," the doctor says to the inspector. "Send a cable to America to learn if such a ship went down?"

The inspector nods. "And you, sir? What is your name?"

The stranger has to think about this for a moment. Part of him doesn't want to recall it. Many memories seem to have walled themselves off. The only thing he needed in recent days was just the instinct to survive.

But the memory is still in there. The remembrance of who he is can be pulled back out if he tries.

Other things—why he was on that ship and what he was doing—will come later. For now, he'll start by regaining his sense of self.

The man closes his eyes, forces the dizziness away, and digs deep. It's like being slapped awake again.

"My name …." He takes another deep breath. "My name is Victor Marius. I remember that I'm an engineer with an American firm, known as Westinghouse. And I'd deeply appreciate your help in contacting my home office. I'm sure they all think that I'm long since dead."

End of Book 2

The Puzzle Box Chronicles is a series, starting with

Book 1

Wreck of the Gossamer.

The Story of Amanda, Jeb, Wayne, Victor, Devlin and others continues in

Those Who Wander

The Puzzle Box Chronicles: Book 3

Shawn P. McCarthy

Made in the USA
Las Vegas, NV
03 February 2024

85239297R00118